Sadie

Thank you, Louise!

First published in Belgium and Holland by Clavis Uitgeverij, Hasselt – Amsterdam, 2016
Copyright © 2016, Clavis Uitgeverij

English translation from the Dutch by Clavis Publishing Inc. New York
Copyright © 2017 for the English language edition: Clavis Publishing Inc. New York

Visit us on the web at www.clavisbooks.com

Beauty and the Beast written and illustrated by An Leysen
Original title: *Belle en het Beest*
Translated from the Dutch by Clavis Publishing

ISBN 978-1-60537-251-8

This book was printed in August 2017 at Publikum d.o.o., Slavka Rodica 6, Belgrade, Serbia

First Edition
10 9 8 7 6 5 4 3 2 1

An Leysen

Beauty and the Beast

Clavis
NEW YORK

There once was a handsome prince,

who was very rich and lived in a beautiful castle.

His heart, however, was made of stone:
He was spoiled and selfish.

One night, an enchantress
paid an unexpected visit to the prince.
She mumbled a curse and changed the prince
into a hideous and fearsome beast.
That was his punishment
for caring about no one but himself.
And he would stay this way
until the day
a girl could love the Beast with all her heart.

The *Beast* lived all by himself in his big castle, in the middle of a large estate. Sometimes he felt so lonely that he roared piteously. His roaring echoed far outside the castle walls. People were so afraid of the Beast that they didn't dare come near the estate, and the Beast never left the grounds. Soon the estate was overgrown and you could hardly see the castle for all the bushes and trees.

So it happened that people forgot all about the Beast.

In a big city, not far from the castle,
lived a rich merchant with his two daughters.
Both of them were pretty and yet they
were as different as night and day.

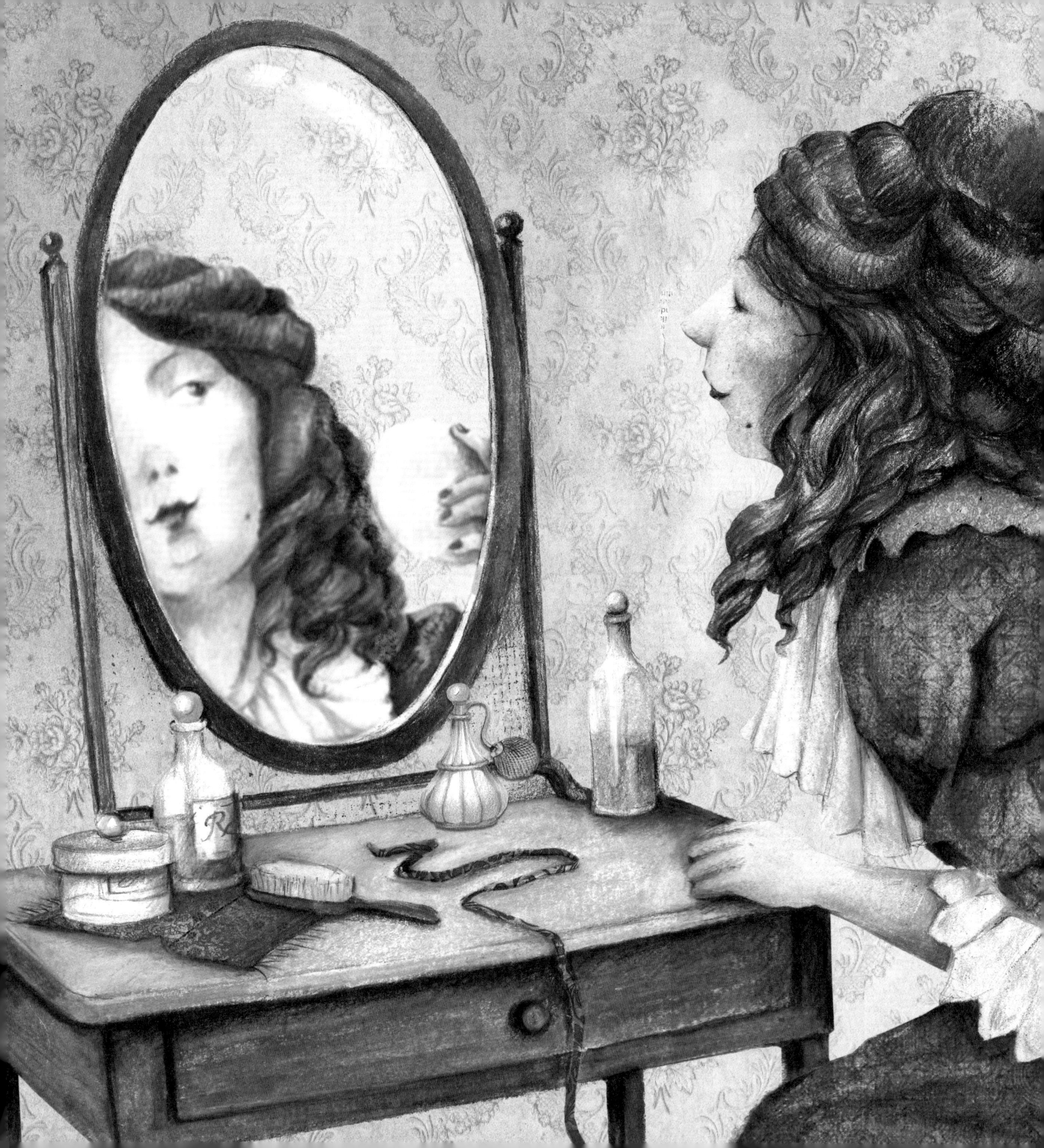

The elder daughter was lazy and insufferable.
She had everything her heart desired but never stopped complaining.
She spent hours of each day gazing at herself in the mirror and trying on
dresses as she got ready for one ball or another.

The elder daughter just didn't understand her younger sister,
who preferred staying at home, keeping her
father company or reading a book.

The younger sister didn't care about expensive clothes or jewelry.
Still, she was by far the prettier of the two.
So pretty, her father always called her *Belle*, which means "beauty."
And soon everyone called her that.

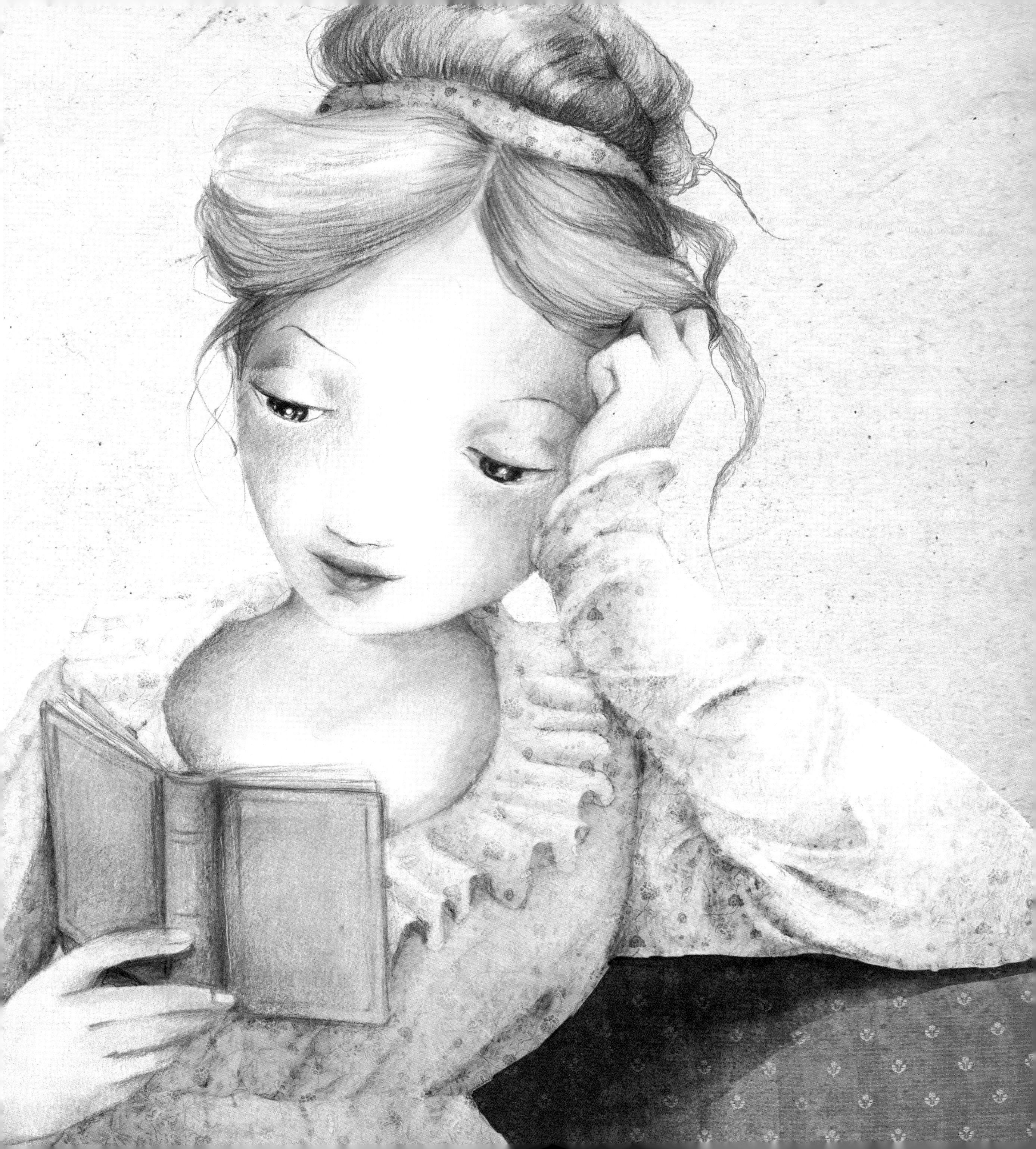

One day, the elder sister finally had something real to complain about; the merchant lost all his money due to misfortune. They had to sell their big, distinguished house in the city and all of their valuable possessions. The servants were let go one by one and the family moved to an ordinary little house in the countryside. The two sisters had to do everything themselves, while their father went looking for work.

Though *Belle* missed her old home, she rolled up her sleeves without complaint, put on an apron, and got to work. She cleaned the house, did the laundry, and made herself useful wherever she could. Meanwhile, her sister sat around and watched. She could only think of her beautiful dresses and the fancy balls she was missing.

Almost a year passed.
Then one day, the merchant was summoned to the city because his uncle had died and left him all his money.

"Oh, Father!" the elder daughter cried, delighted. "When you're in the city, you can buy me new dresses of silk and velvet. And jewelry! And matching shoes!" She was convinced they were going to move back to their big house in the city and all those expensive things could be hers again.

The merchant nodded and asked his younger daughter, "What about you, my dear Belle? What do you want?"
"I don't need anything, Father. The only thing I want is for you to come home soon."
Both girls said goodbye to their father and he left for the city right away.

It was a long journey. The merchant was traveling on horseback for four days. But when he came to the city, it turned out that his uncle hadn't left him much money. There wasn't even enough to buy the things his elder daughter had asked for.

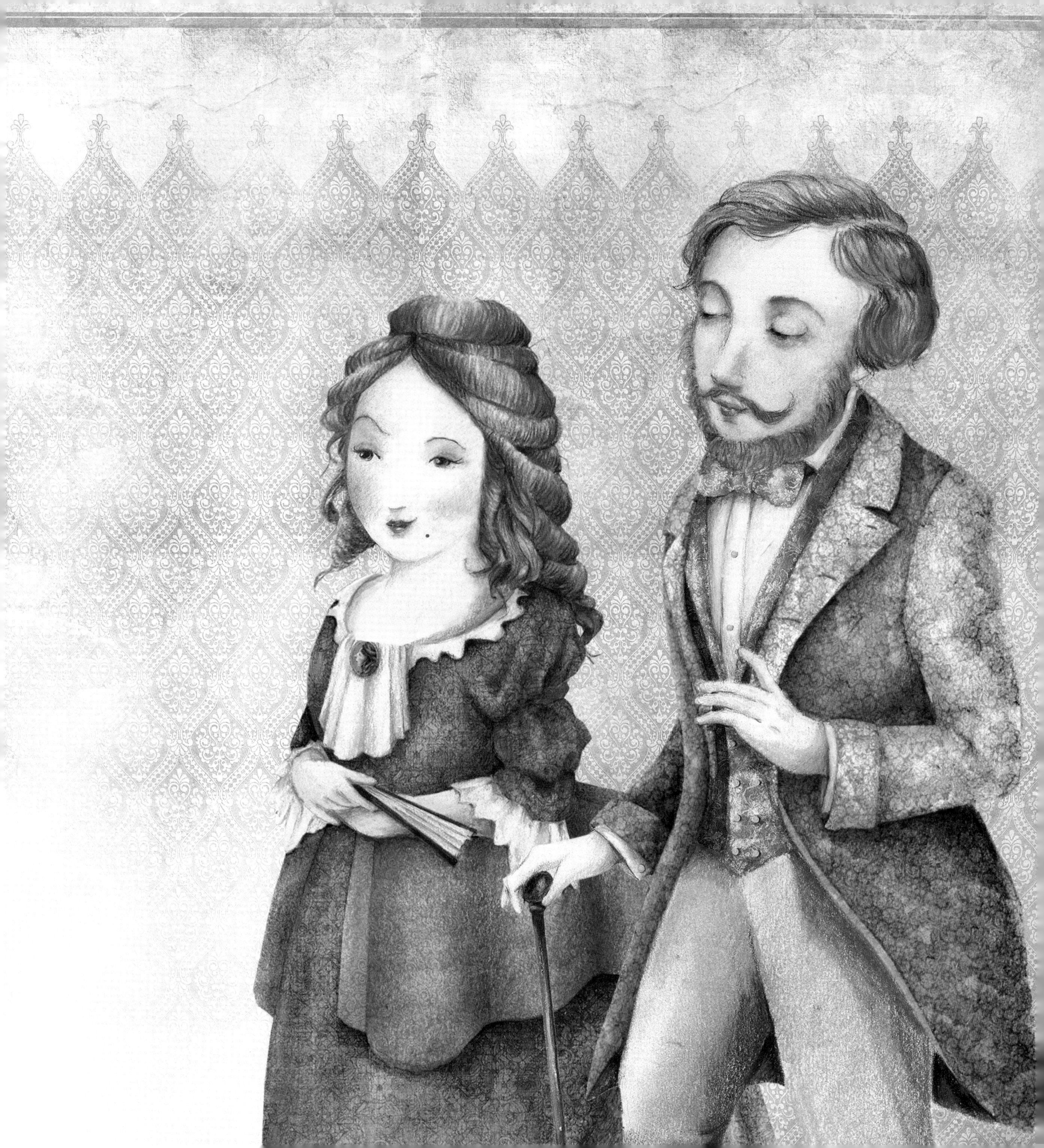

With a heavy heart, the merchant left the city.

It started to snow harder and harder and he lost his way in the storm. When night fell, the poor man thought he might die of hunger and cold. Suddenly he saw a light in the distance. He hurried toward it and came upon a castle with brightly lit windows. With his last bit of strength he banged on the big front doors.

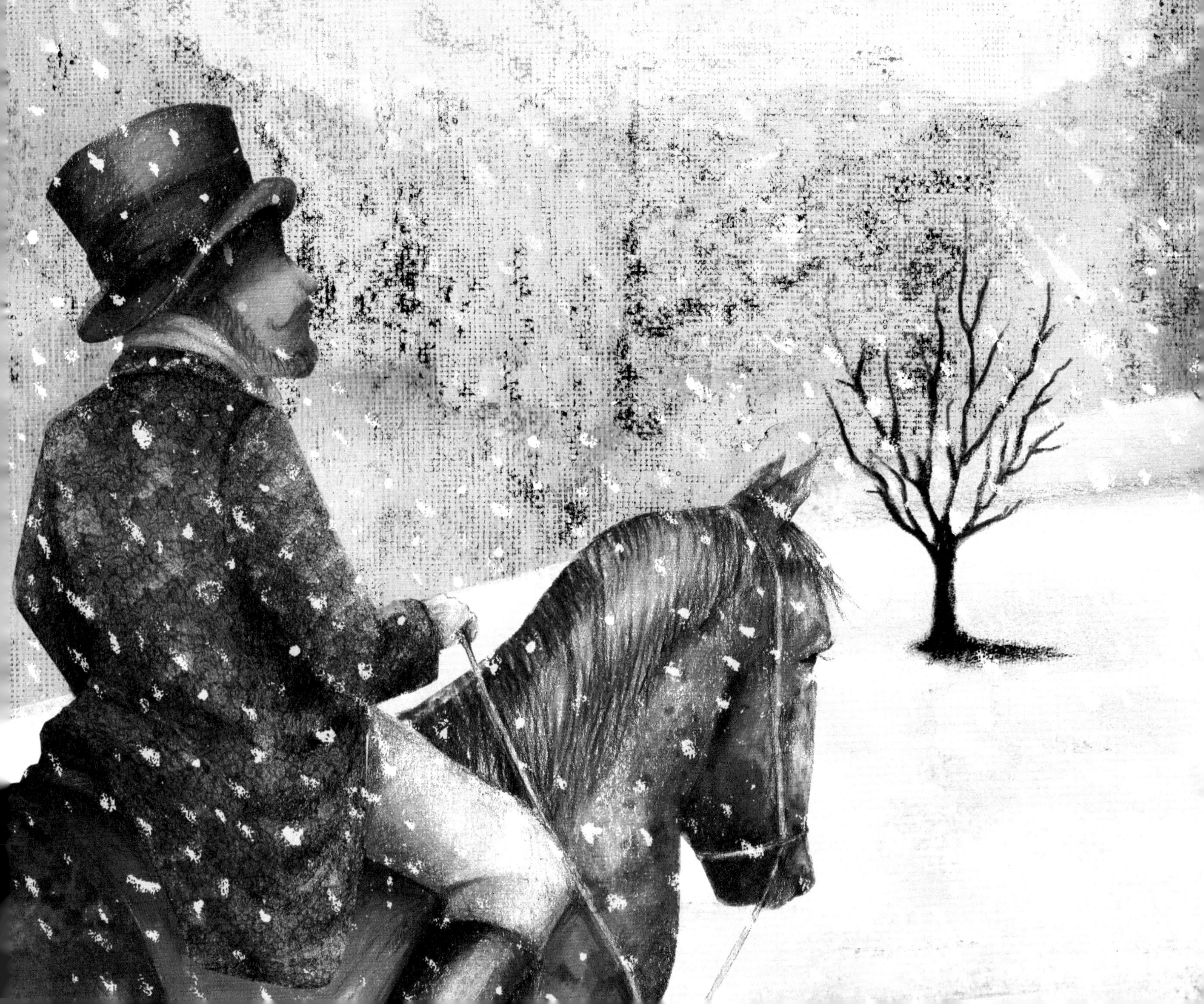

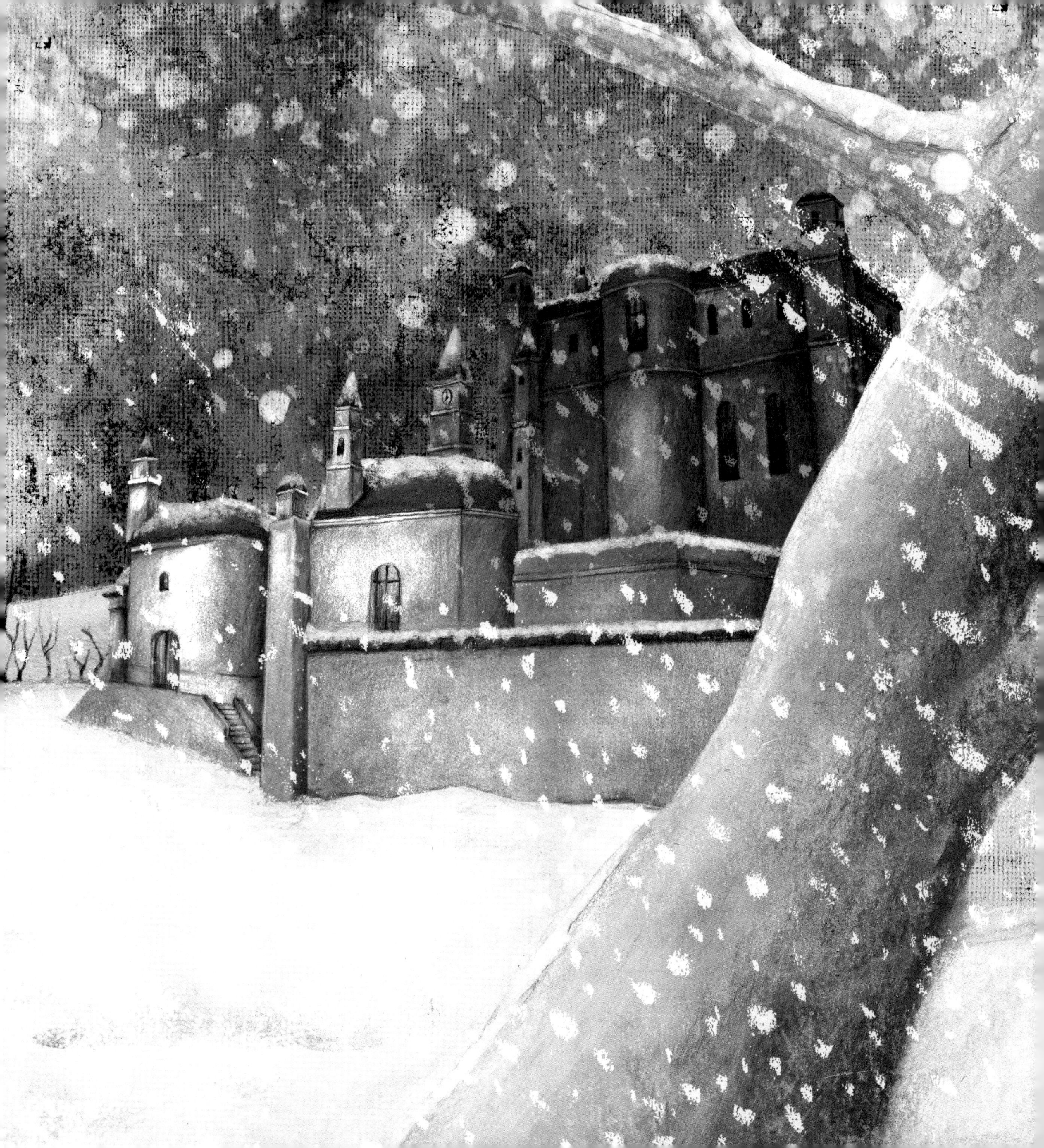

The heavy doors swung open with a groan.
The merchant saw no one and continued in until he found a big room where a warm fire was crackling in the fireplace. There was a table filled with delicious dishes. It all looked so inviting and the man was so hungry that he plopped down on a chair and helped himself to the food and drink. After a while, he fell asleep with a half-full glass still in his hand.

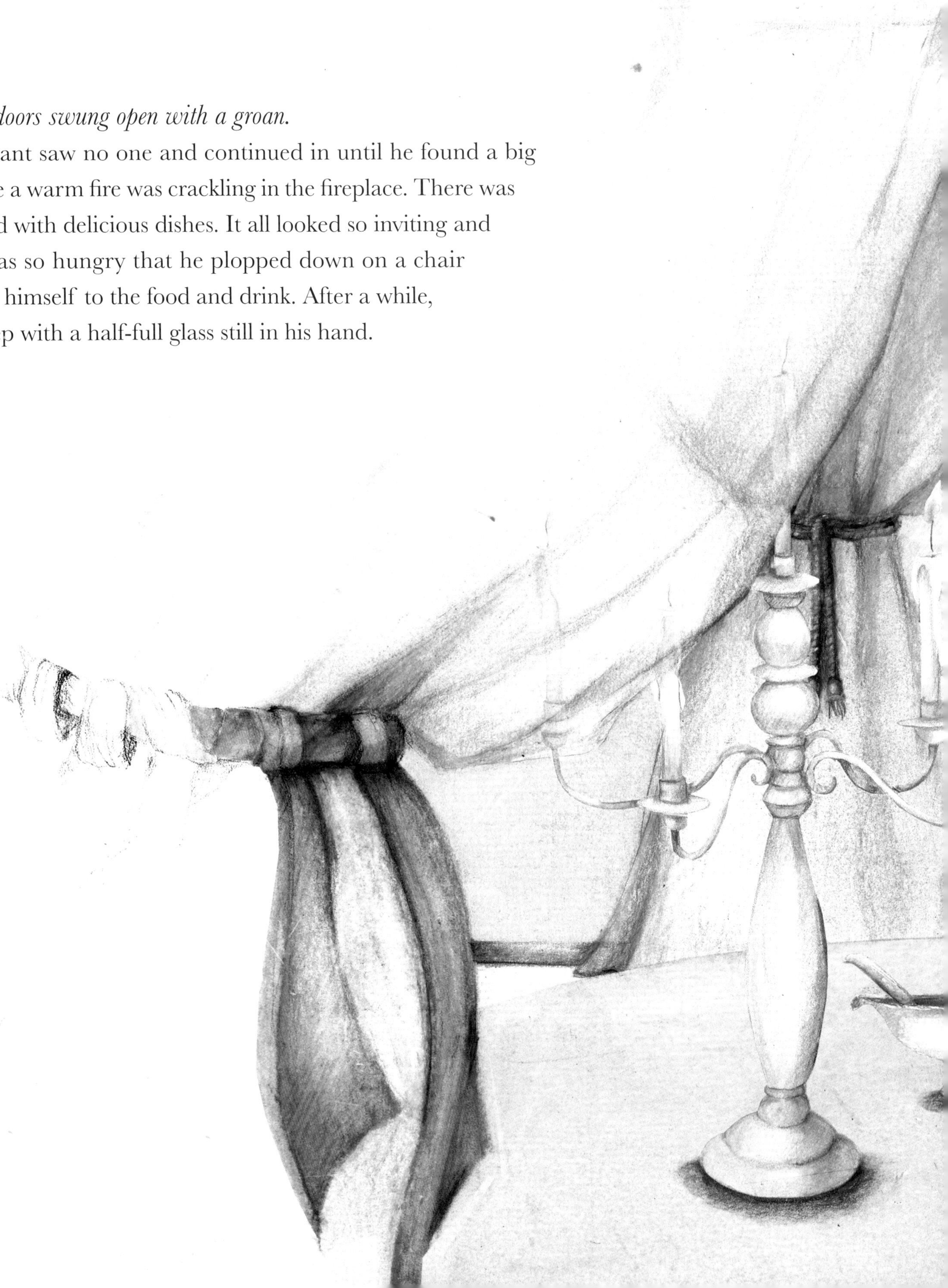

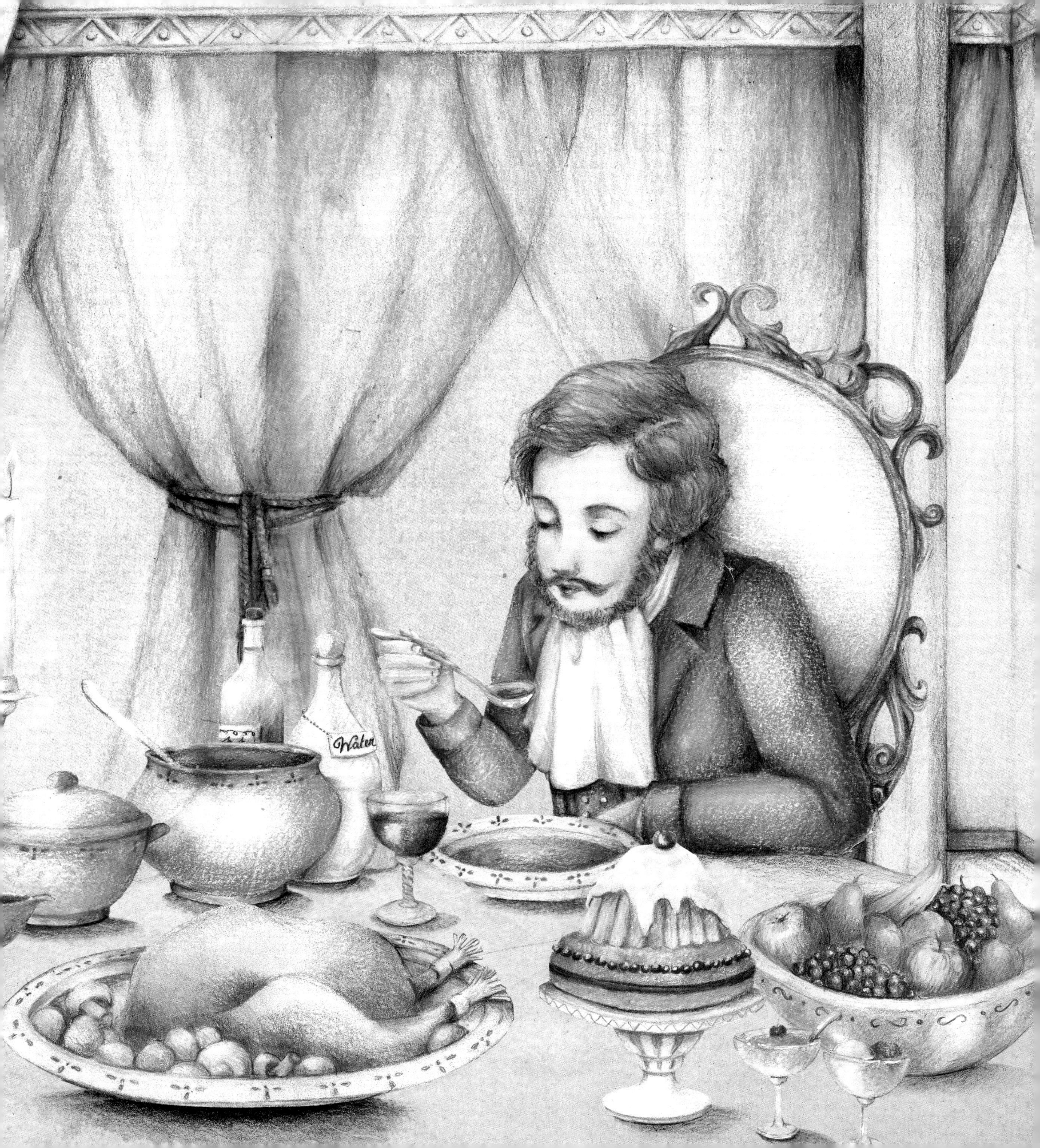
Water

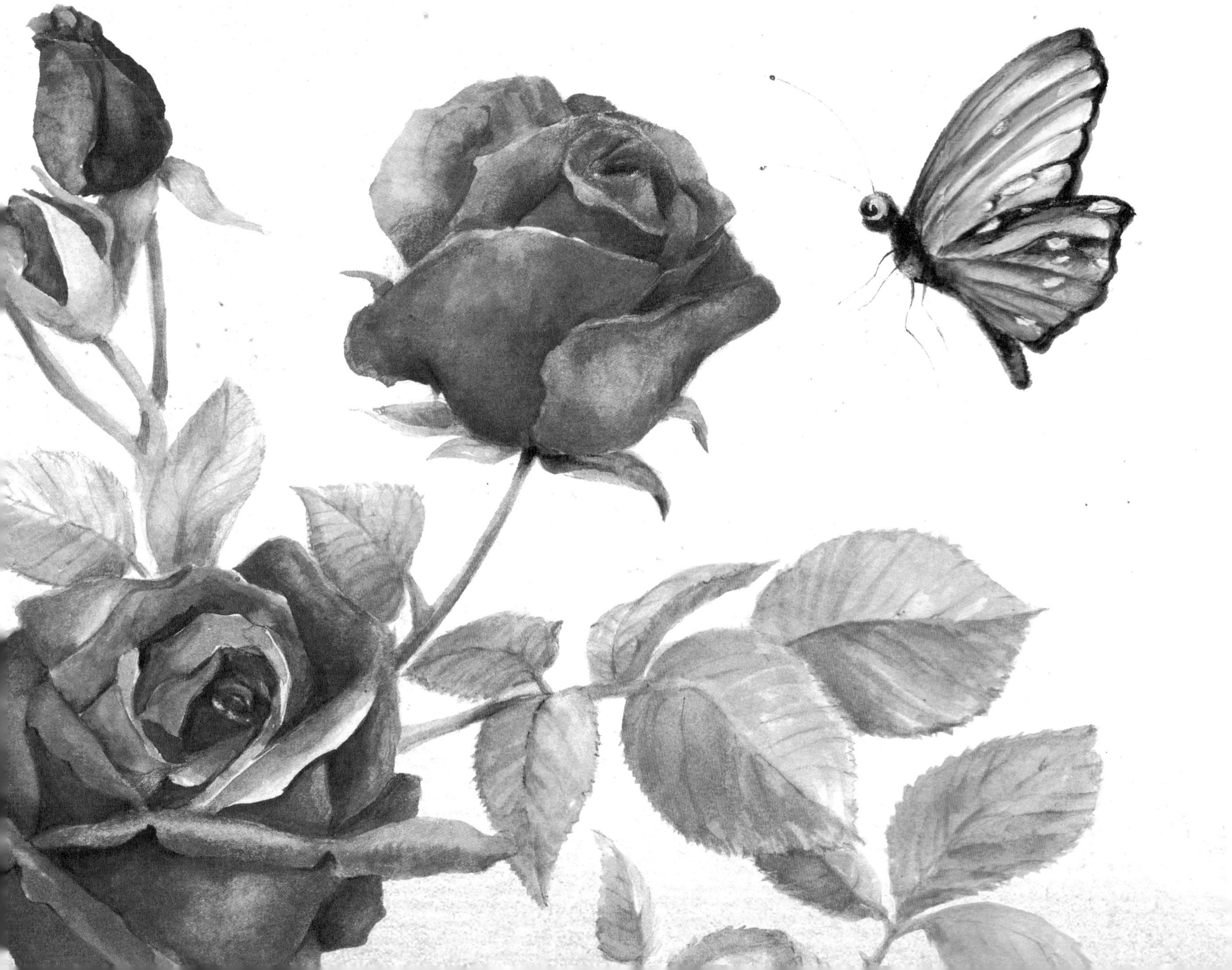

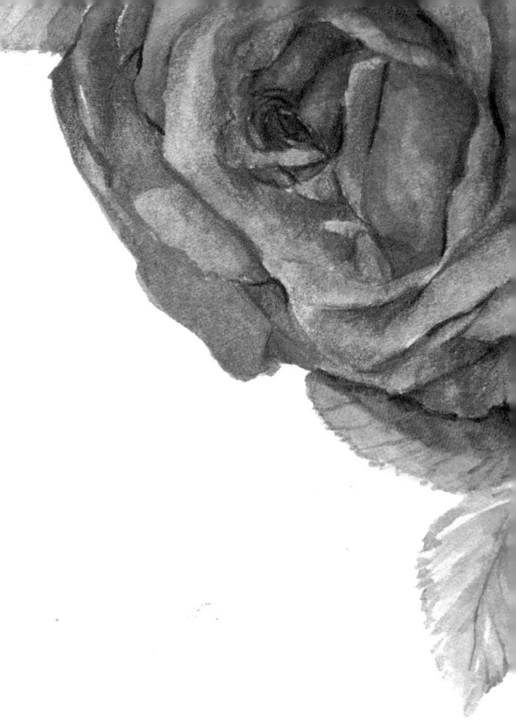

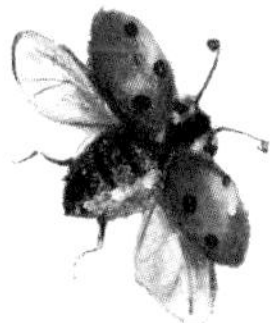

It was almost noon when the merchant was awoken by the sun on his face. Confused, he looked around; he was no longer sitting at the table, but lay in a nice soft bed. His clothes hung over a chair, washed and ironed.

"This must be the castle of a good fairy," the man mumbled to himself. "She probably took pity on me after all my misfortunes." He quickly got dressed and went outside to look for his horse.

The merchant was thunderstruck when he saw that the trees and bushes in the castle garden had green leaves. Colorful flowers bloomed and insects buzzed under a radiant sun, while in the distance he could see the wintry forest where he'd lost his way the night before. *Good heavens! My daughters will never believe me,* the merchant thought. *I'll bring them a flower, so they can see for themselves.* He had stooped to pick a rose, when suddenly a huge shadow blocked the sun.

Startled, the merchant turned around and looked into the furious eyes of the most fearsome monster he had ever seen.

"Ungrateful man!" the monster roared, so loud it made the ground shake. "I gave you shelter when you were lost, I fed you and let you sleep in my own bed, and as thanks you steal flowers from my garden. Those roses are more precious to me than all my possessions. *You will pay for this!*"

Shocked and terrified, the merchant shook like a leaf in the wind.

"Have mercy!" he begged. "Please don't hurt me! I didn't mean to upset you. I just wanted to take a rose as a gift to my daughters."

The Beast thought for a while, then narrowed his eyes and growled: "All right! I'll let you live, on one condition: One of your daughters must take your place in this castle."

Of course the merchant would never send one of his daughters to the Beast, but he wanted to see them one more time, and so he agreed.

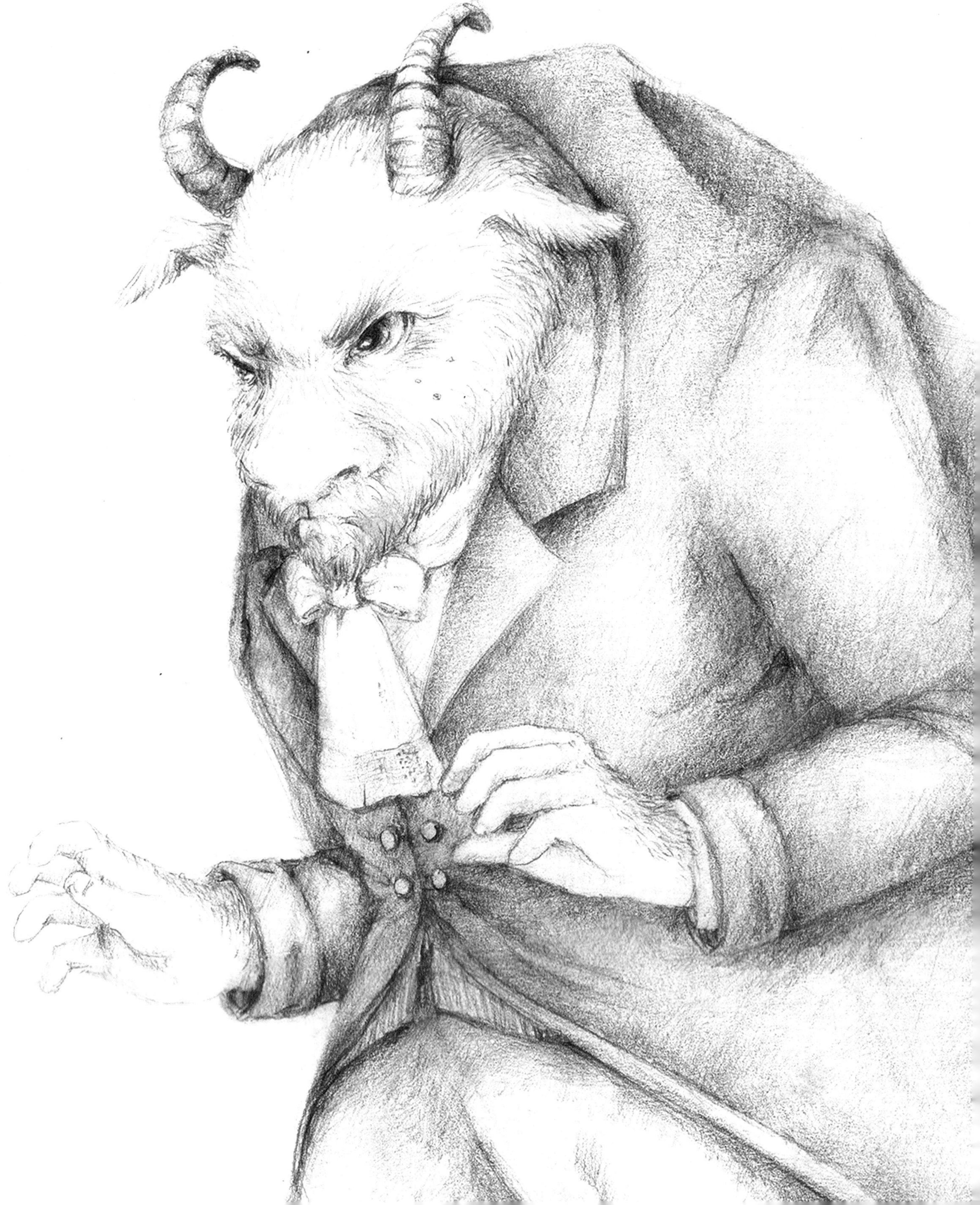

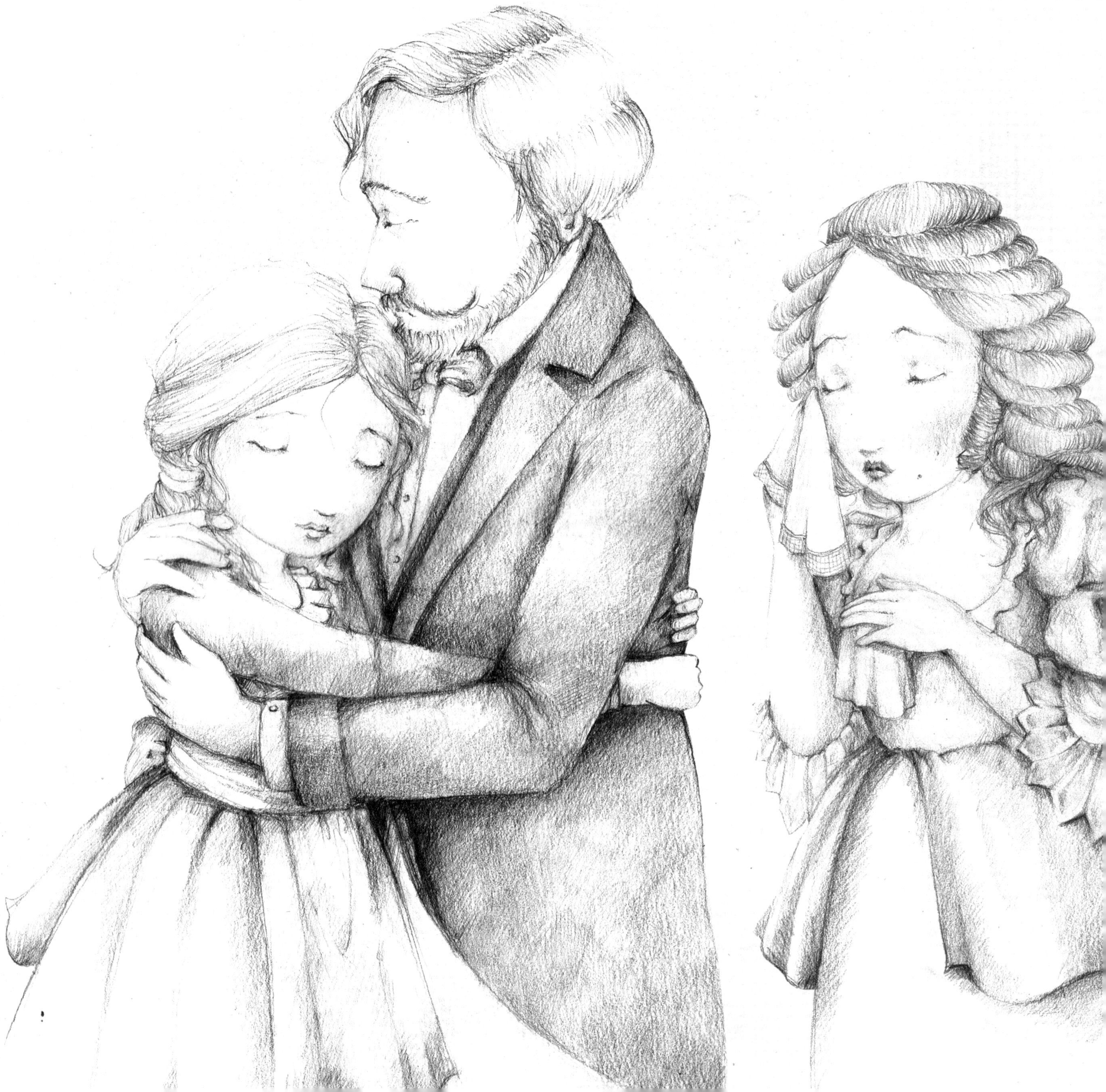

Now that it was light and the snowstorm was over, the man easily found his way home. He was still shaking when he told his daughters about his misadventure. The two sisters burst into tears–Belle because her father had to go through such a horrible experience, and her sister because there still wasn't money for new dresses.

Belle gave her father a hug and said, "Father, I don't mind taking your place in the castle. If it's really as beautiful as you described it, that Beast can't be all bad."

And though her father tried to stop her, *Belle* left that same night for the *Beast's* castle.

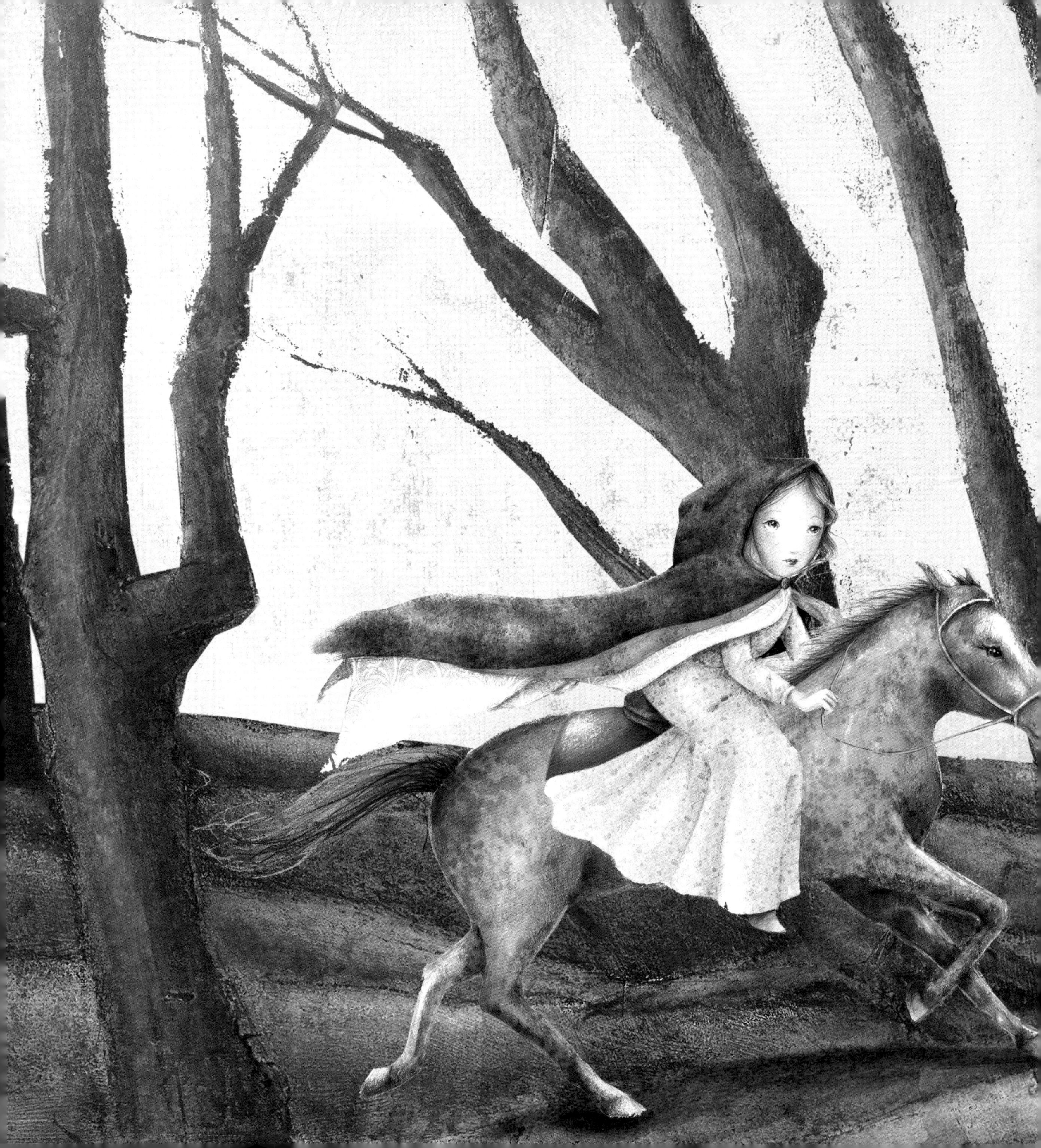

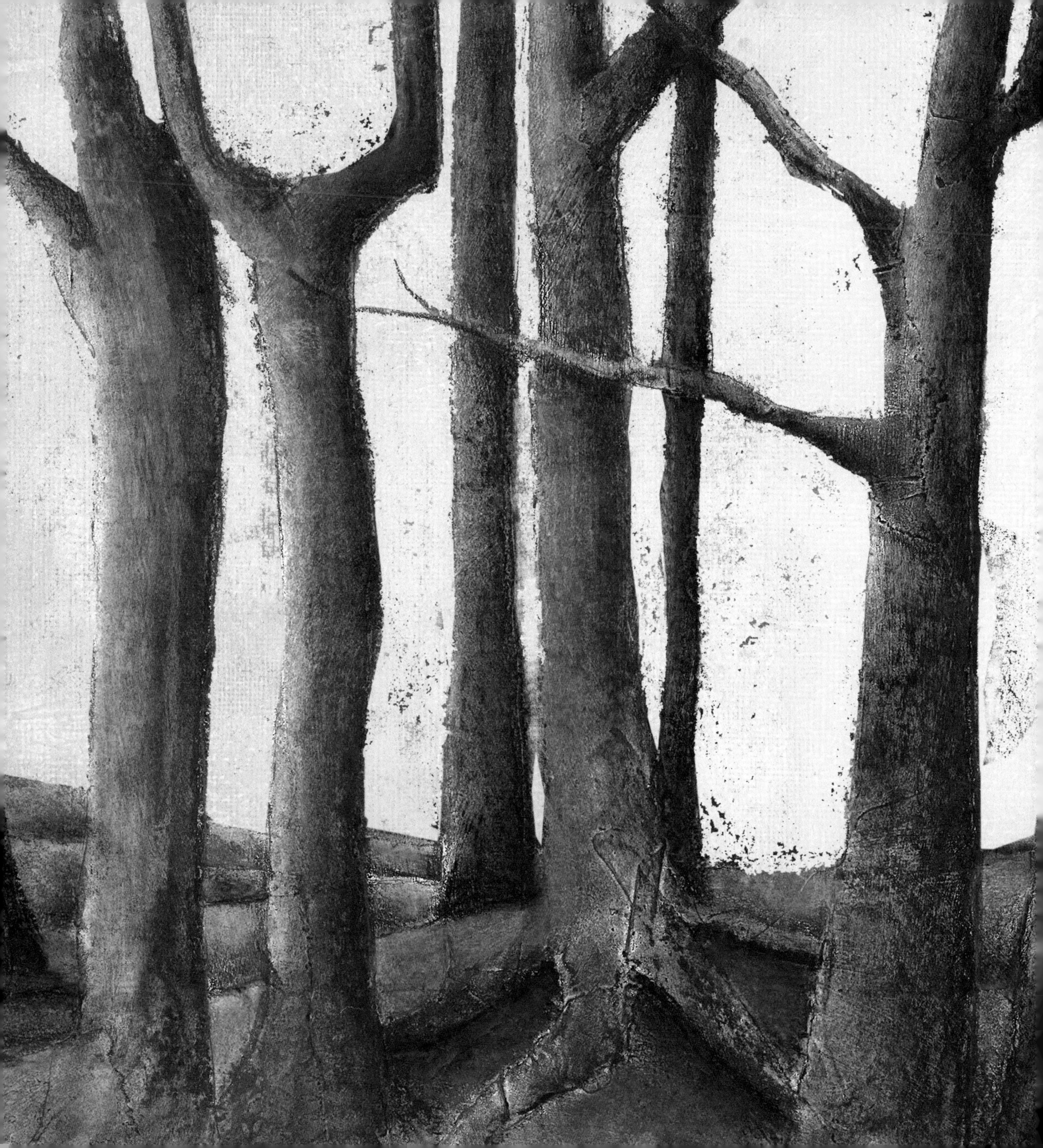

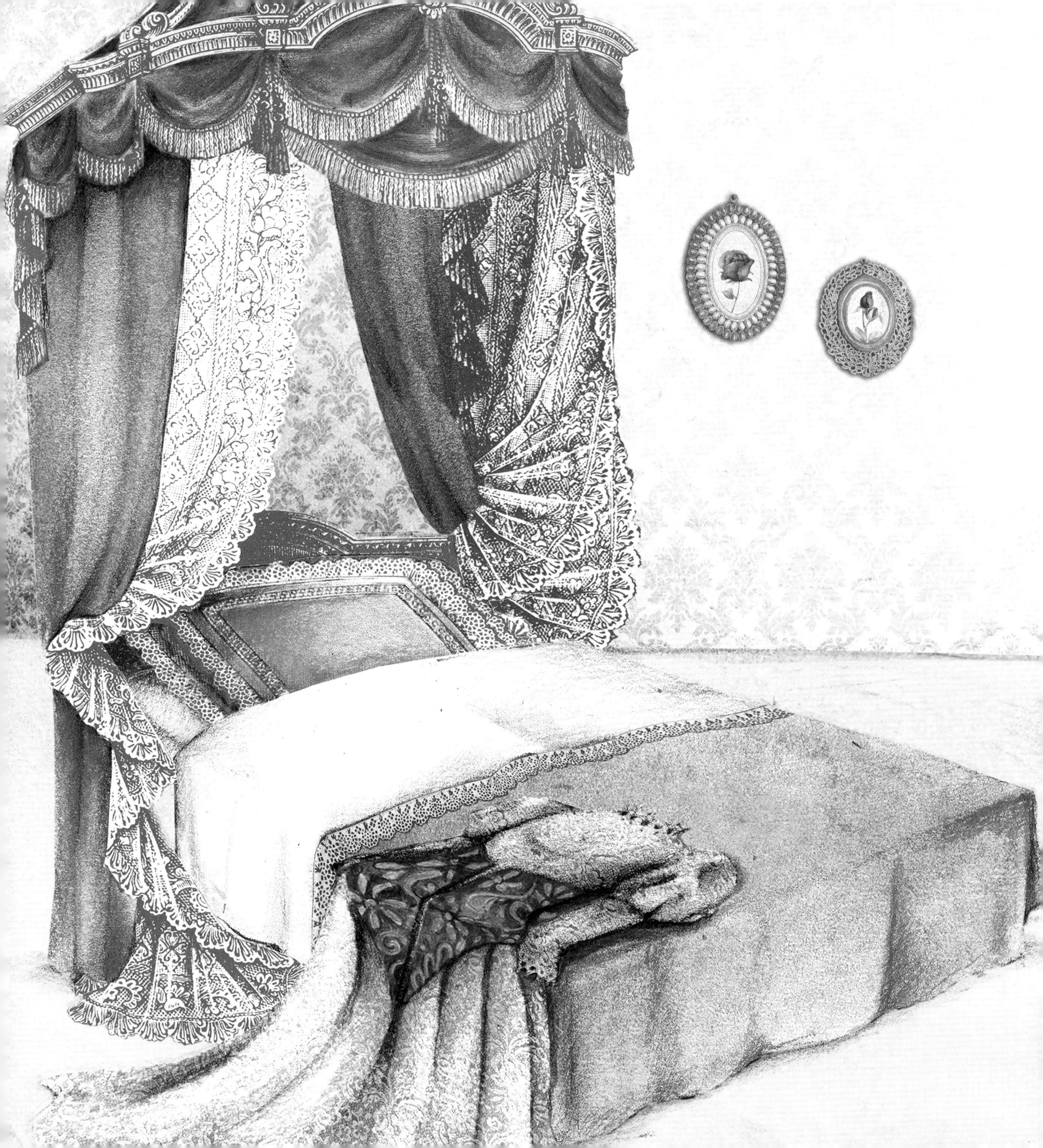

It was all exactly as her father had described.
When Belle knocked on the high castle doors, they opened by
themselves. Inside the big hall, a snug fire was burning and the
dining room table was richly set. But there was no one in sight.
Belle wandered through the rooms and halls of the castle. She
went from one discovery to the next. It was all so magical it made
her dizzy. Suddenly she stopped in front of a door with her
name written on it in graceful golden letters:

Belle

Carefully, the girl opened the door and entered the room.
It was a beautiful room with a huge four-poster bed in the
center. On the bed lay the prettiest dress Belle had ever
seen: as blue as the sky in summer and made out of lace.
While she admired herself in the mirror, Belle suddenly
heard loud thumping. *Heavy footsteps thundered through
the hallway and the next moment he was standing in
front of her…*

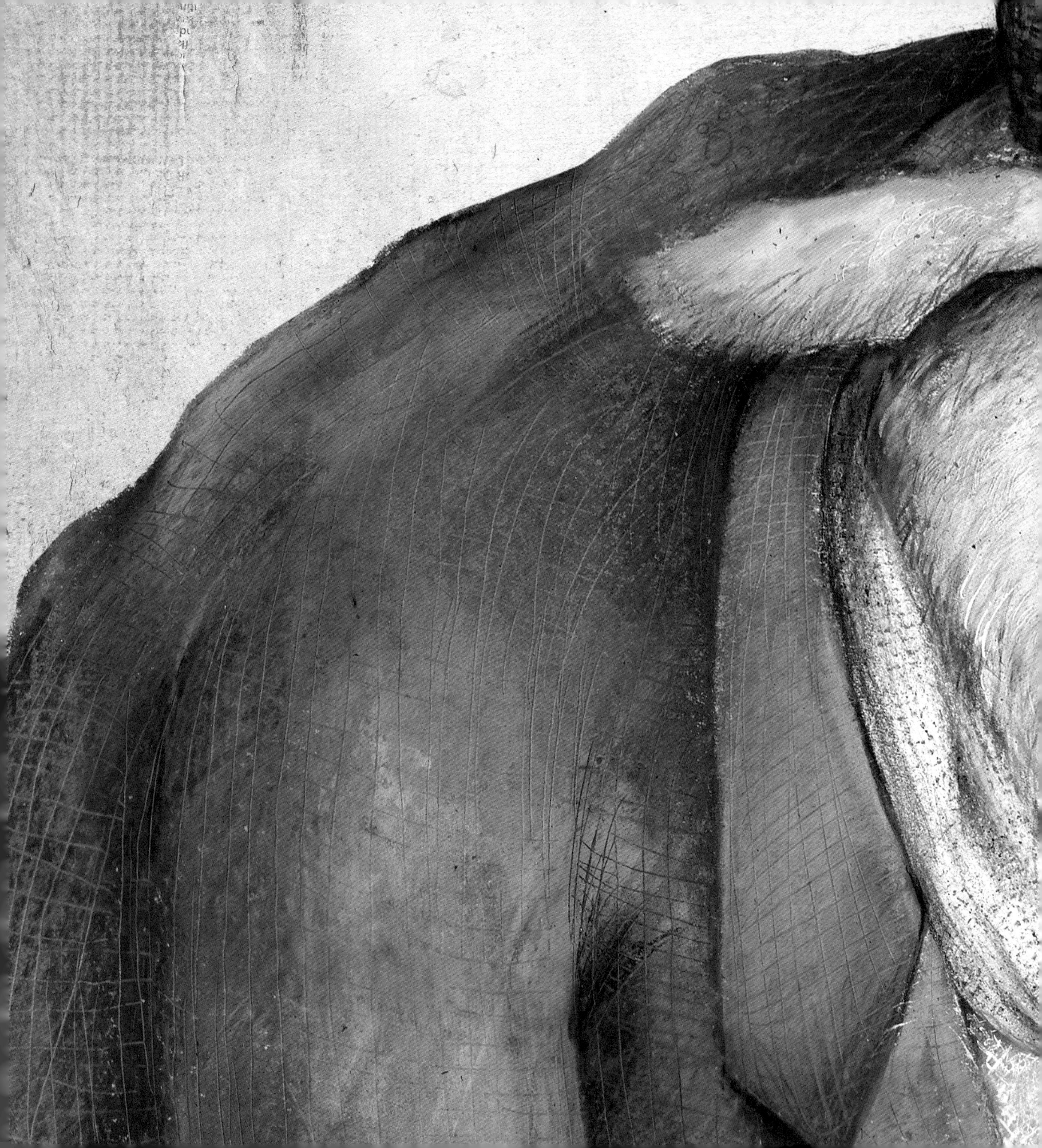

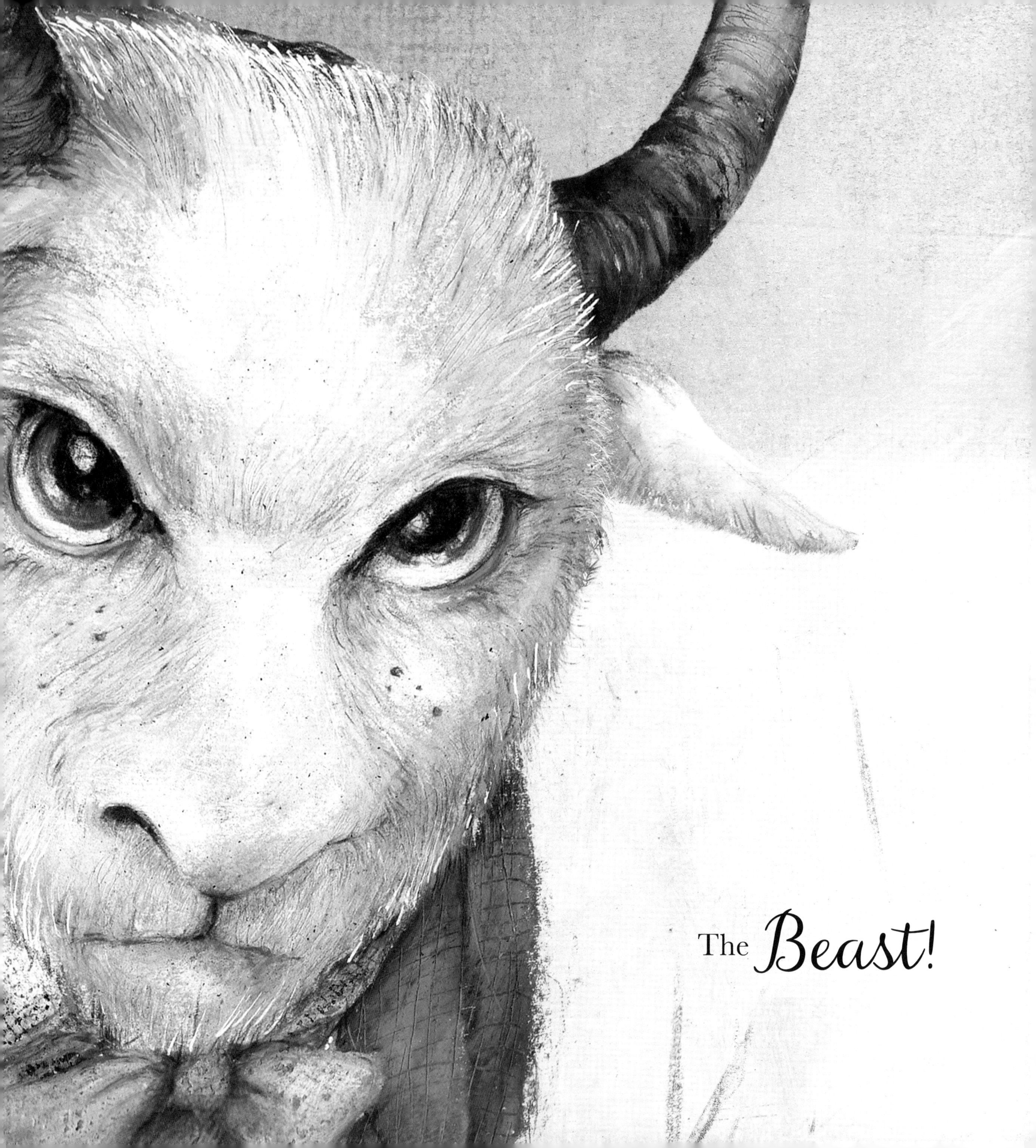

The *Beast!*

Belle couldn't believe what she saw.
The Beast was huge!

He was more terrifying than Belle had even imagined. "Don't be scared, Belle!"
the Beast grumbled. "I won't hurt you. In this castle, you are my queen."

To Belle's relief, the Beast didn't show himself again during the next few days.
But one night, just when Belle was about to eat dinner, he suddenly appeared.
He looked frightful! "Can I sit with you while you eat?" he asked gruffly.
"If you don't like my company, I'll leave."

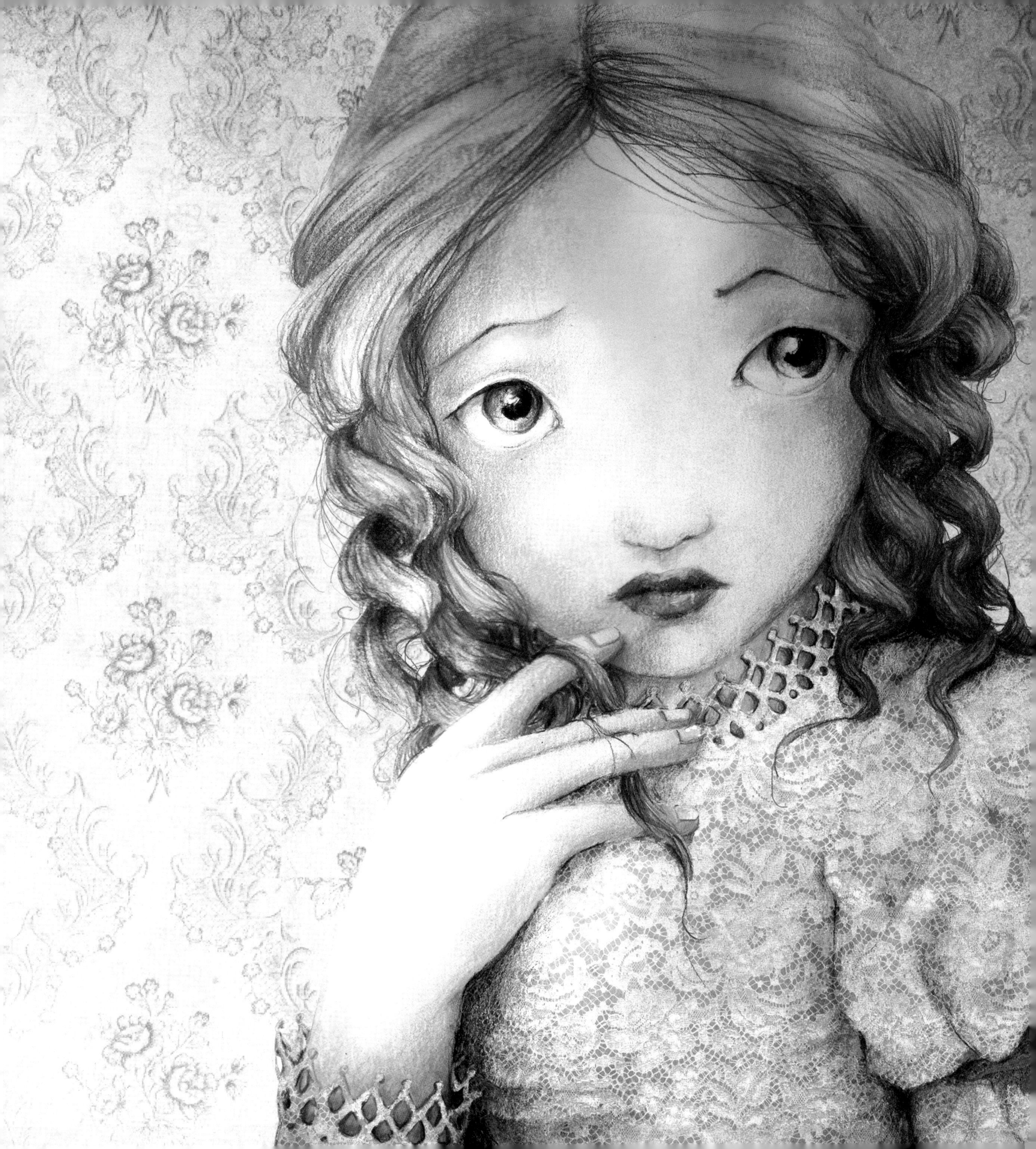

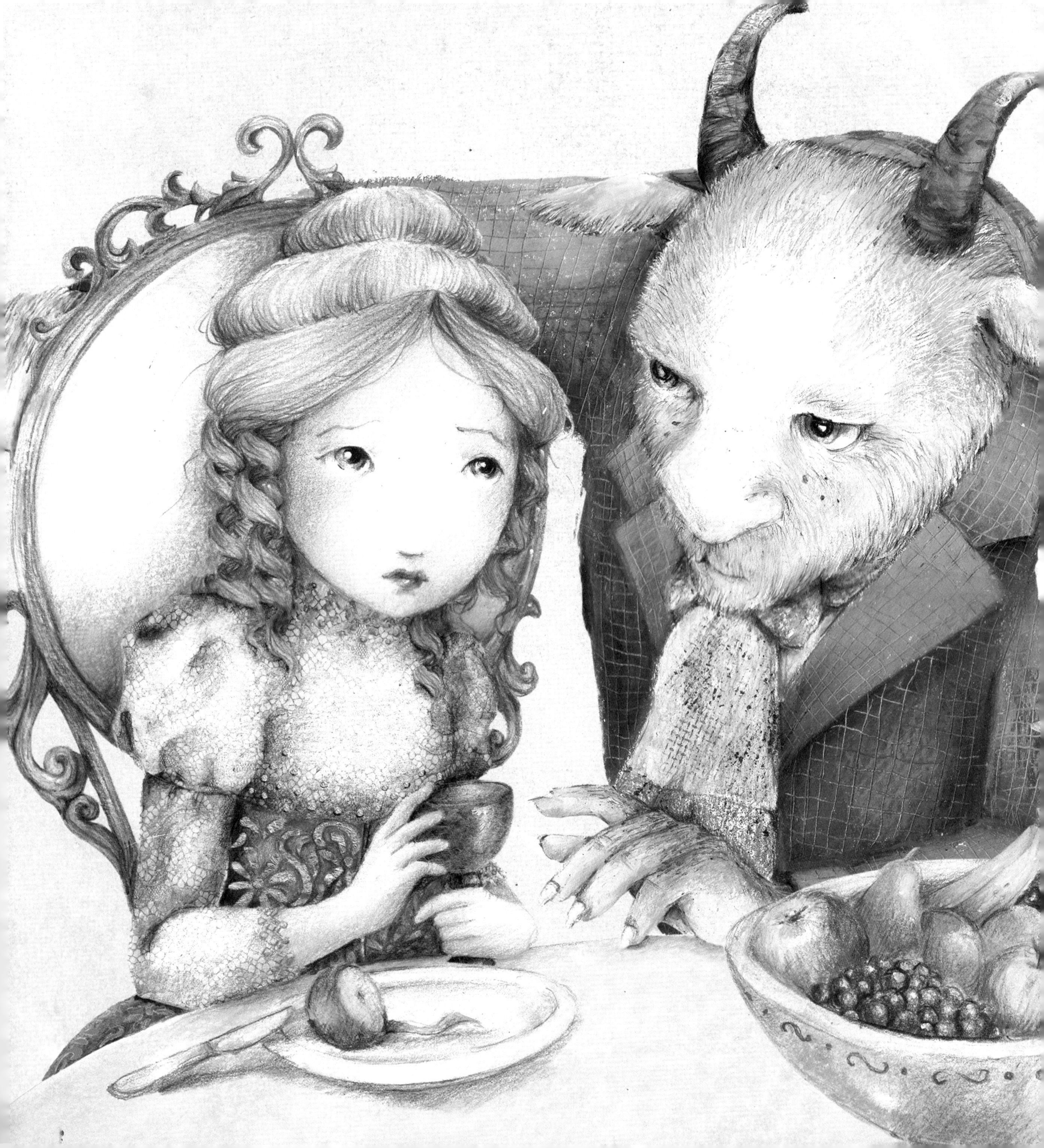

Belle was afraid of the Beast and she preferred not to have him around, but when she looked in his big, sad eyes, she didn't have the heart to send him away. To her surprise, the Beast was very kind. He tried his very best to make her comfortable. Belle almost forgot to be scared of him. When the Beast finally got up to leave, he surprised her again. "Belle, I know I'm ugly, but I'm falling in love with you. Will you marry me?"

"No!" the girl cried, appalled. *"I could never marry a beast."*
With tears in her eyes, she fled to her room.

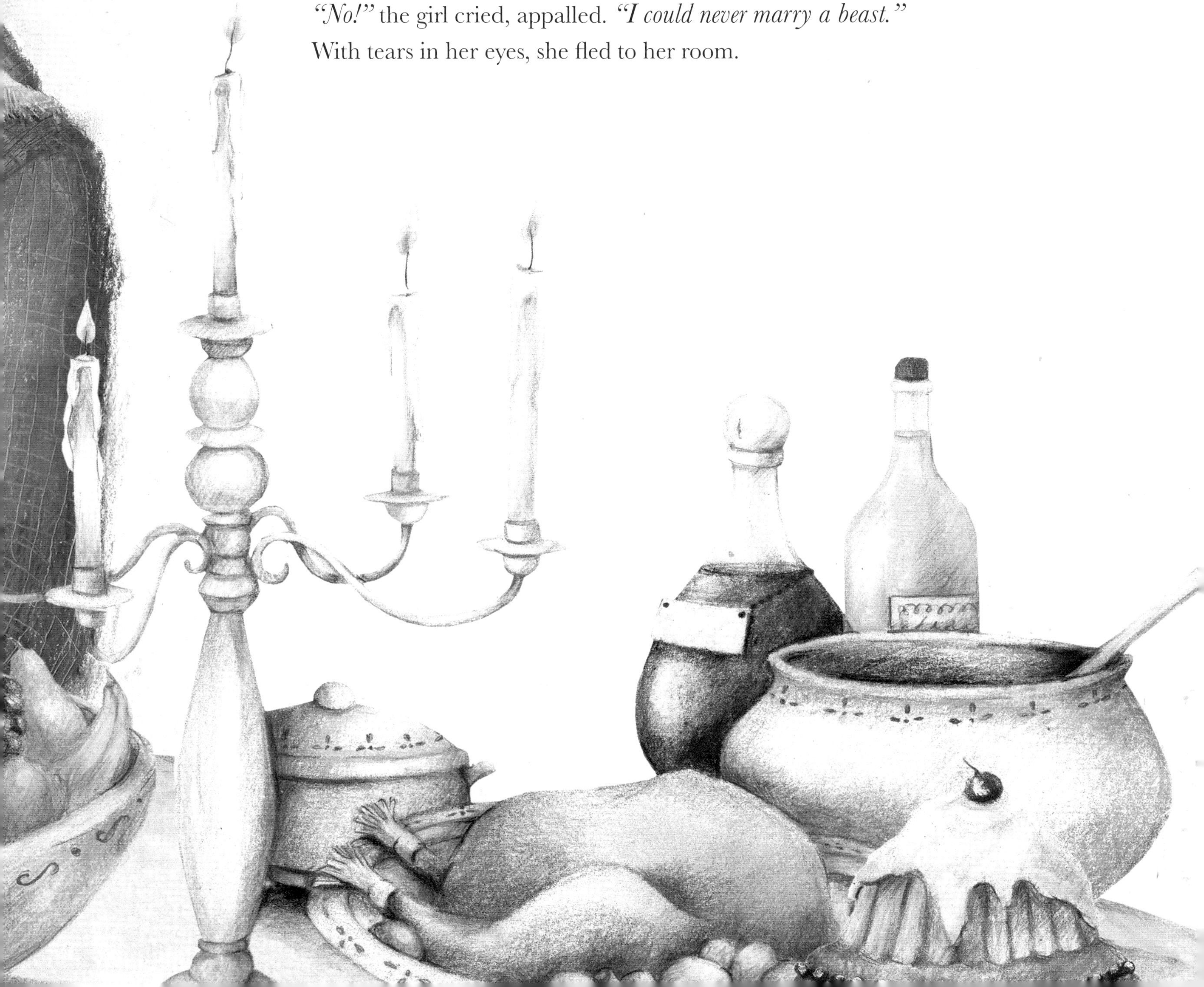

The seasons passed. Spring came and then summer. Belle felt at home in the castle. During the day, she read a book or went for a walk in the enchanted garden. But she especially looked forward to the nights. Then the castle was filled with magic. Candles burned everywhere and soft music played. Belle's every wish was fulfilled. It was as if invisible hands served her, because she never saw anyone but the Beast.

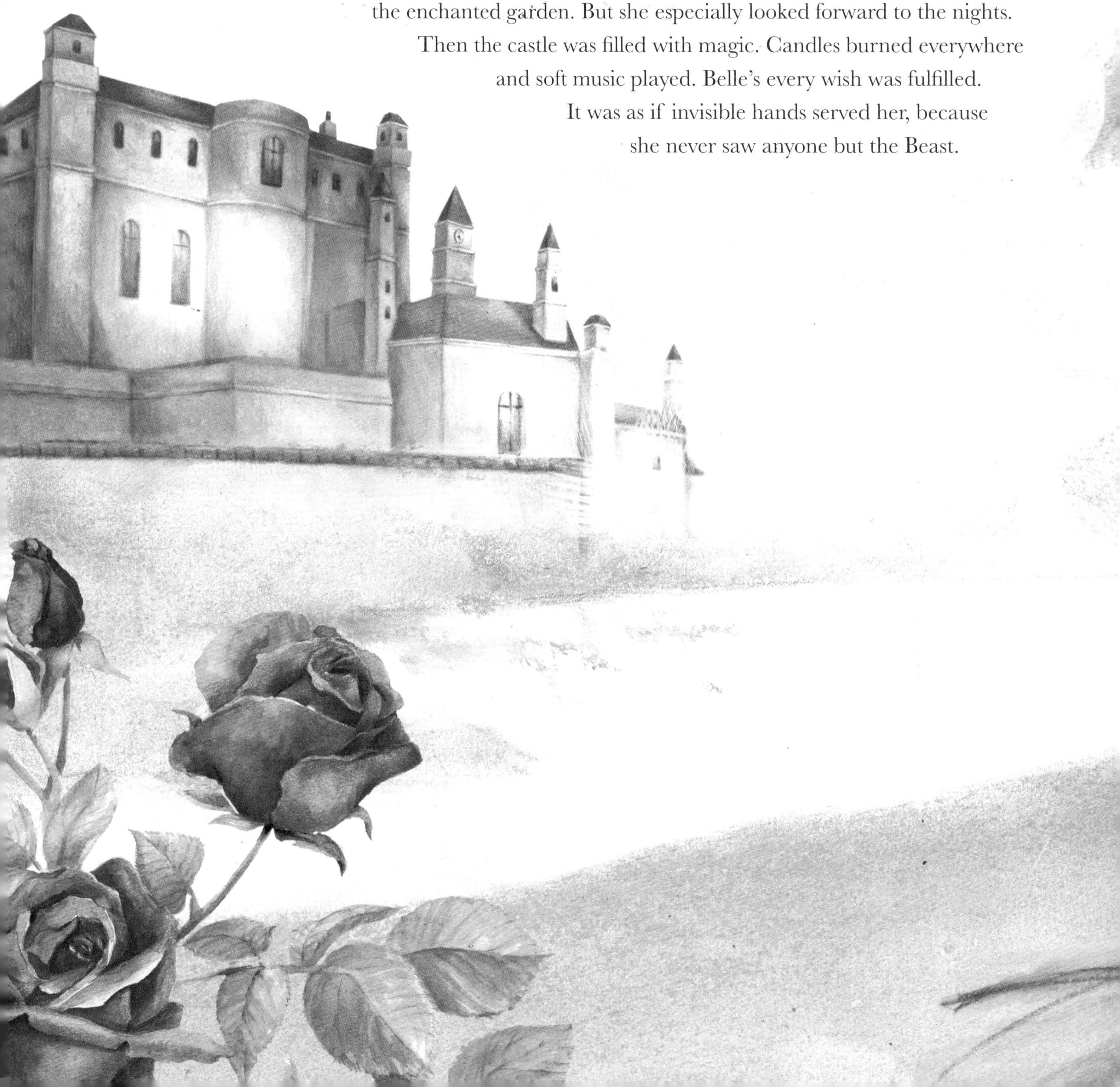

He came to visit her every night.
And every time, Belle discovered another good thing about him. Instead of dreading his visits, she started counting the minutes: when the clock struck seven, the Beast appeared. Then they talked and laughed or danced through the halls of the castle. When they were together, time flew by and Belle felt happier than she'd ever been.

But one thing troubled her. Every evening before he left her, the Beast asked her again if she would marry him, and he let out a disappointed sigh every time she answered: *"No, Beast."*

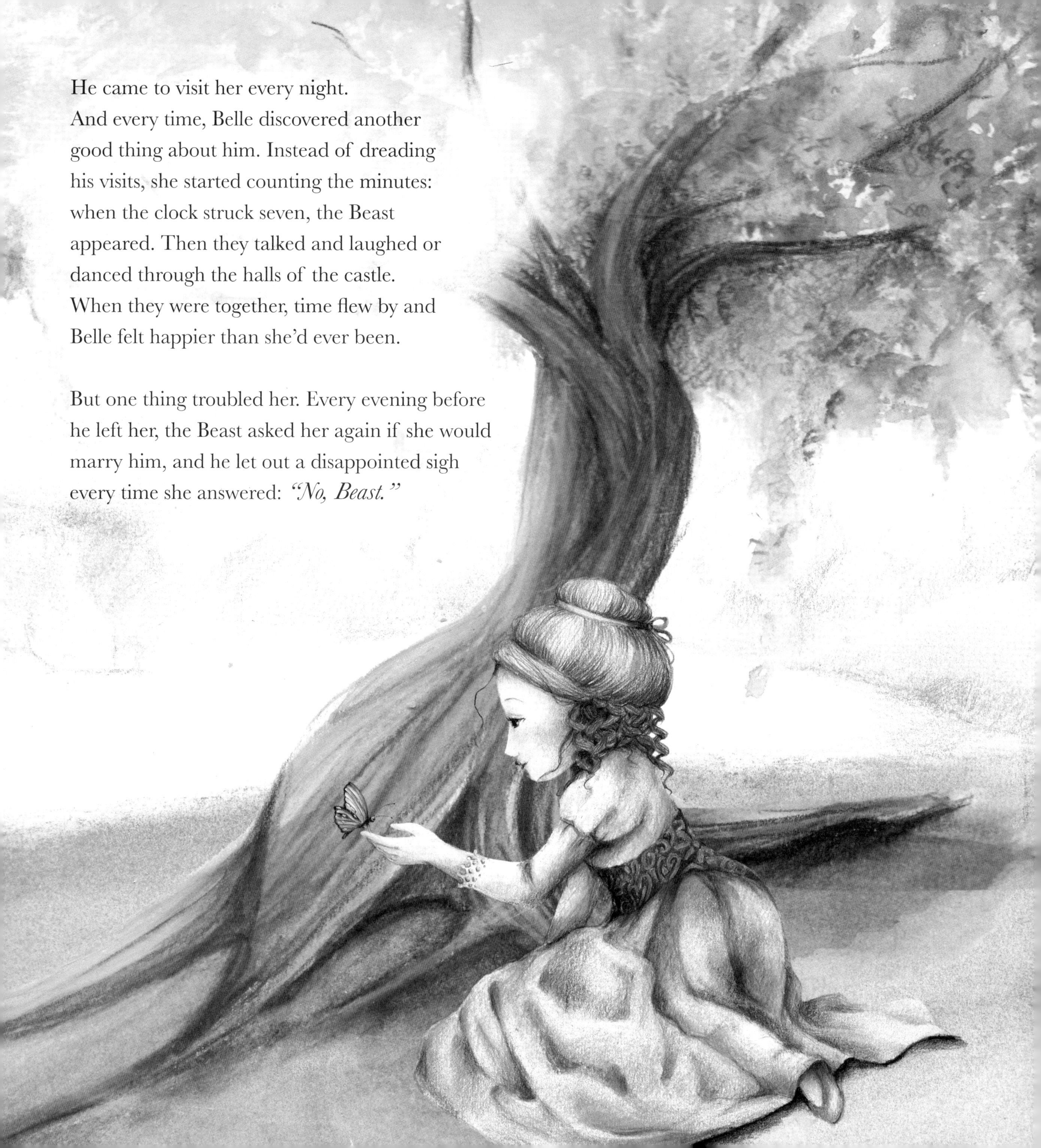

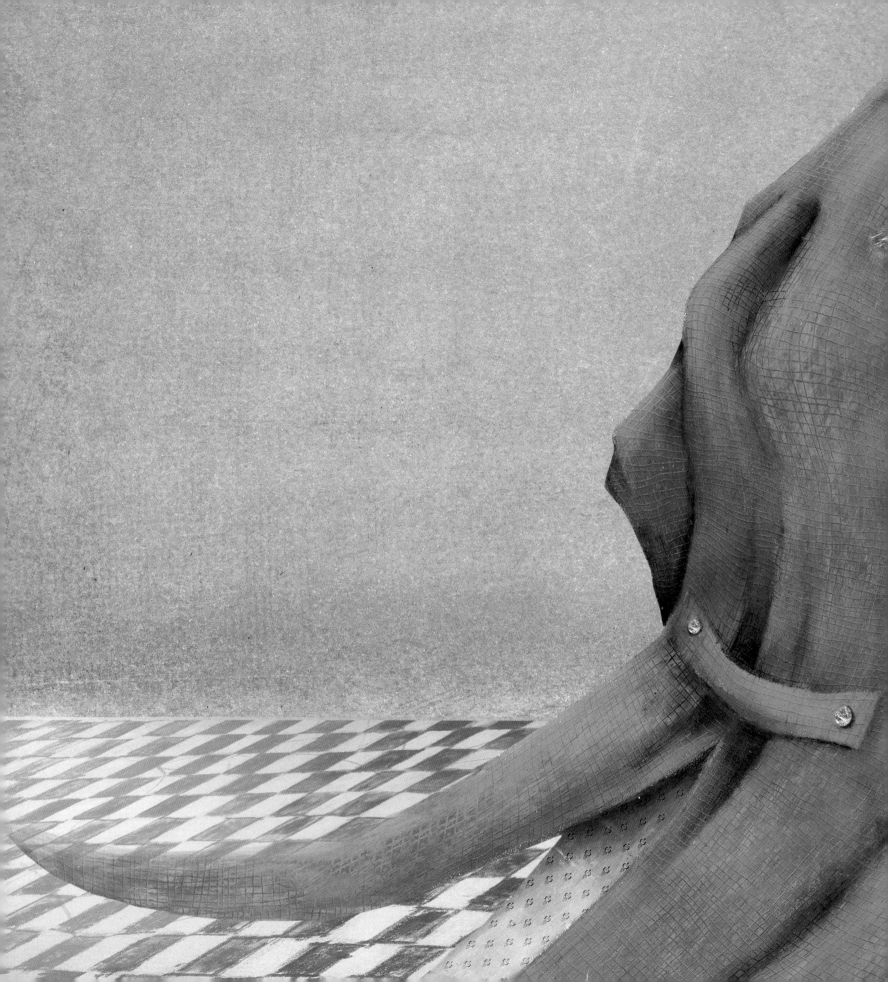

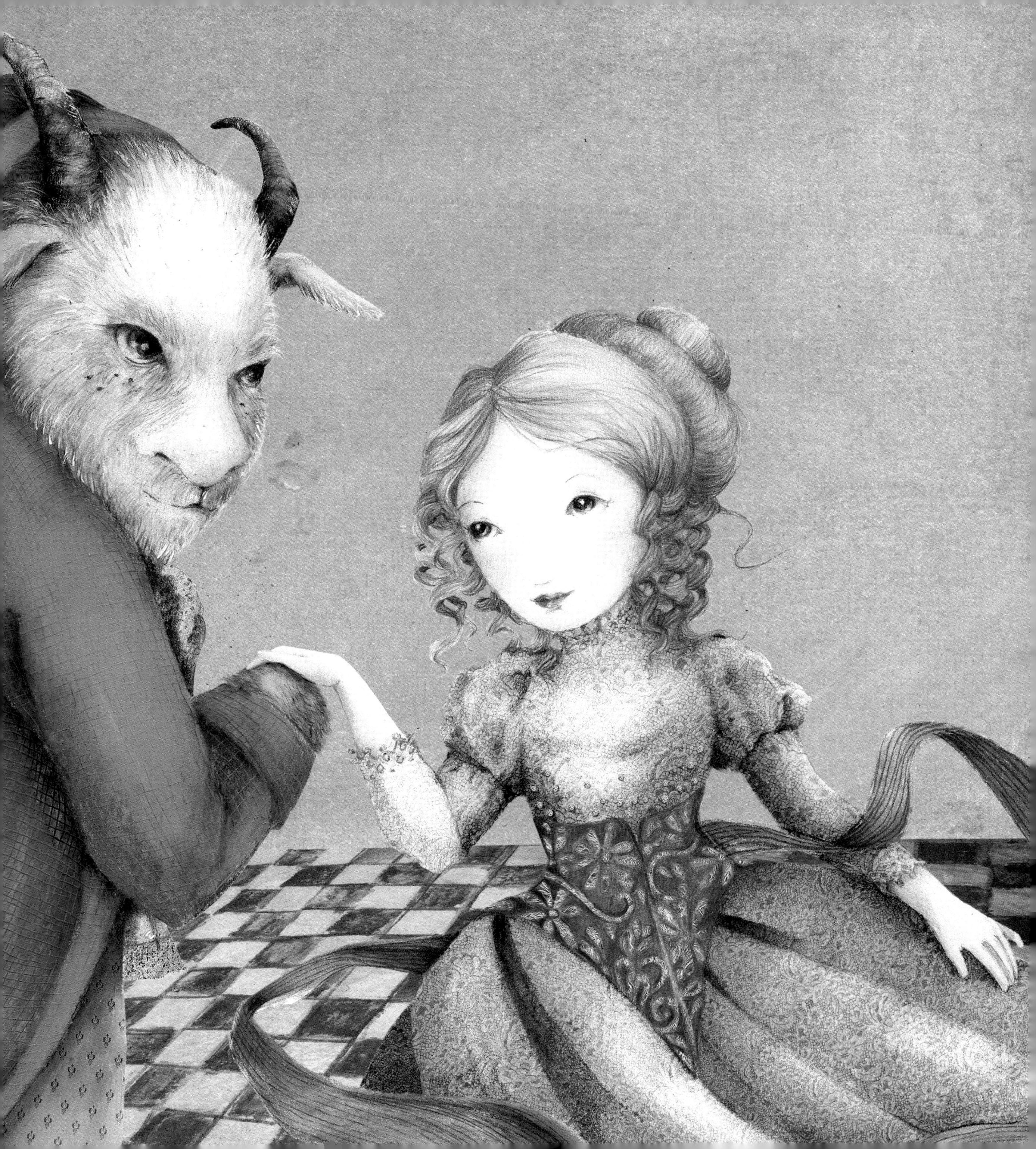

One day, the Beast surprised Belle with an enchanted mirror.
"Here," he said softly. "Now you won't have to feel lonely during the day."
The girl gave a little cry of wonder when she saw not her own reflection in
the mirror, but instead her house and her father and sister.

Belle was so happy with the mirror that she would stare in it for hours. She
soon noticed that her father looked worse every day. One day, the Beast
found Belle crying with the mirror in her hand. "What's wrong, my dear
Belle?" he asked, worried.

"It's my father. He's sick with worry about me. Please let me go to him."
For the first time since she'd met the Beast, he roared angrily at her.
"NO! You can't leave this castle. EVER!" He marched away in a rage.

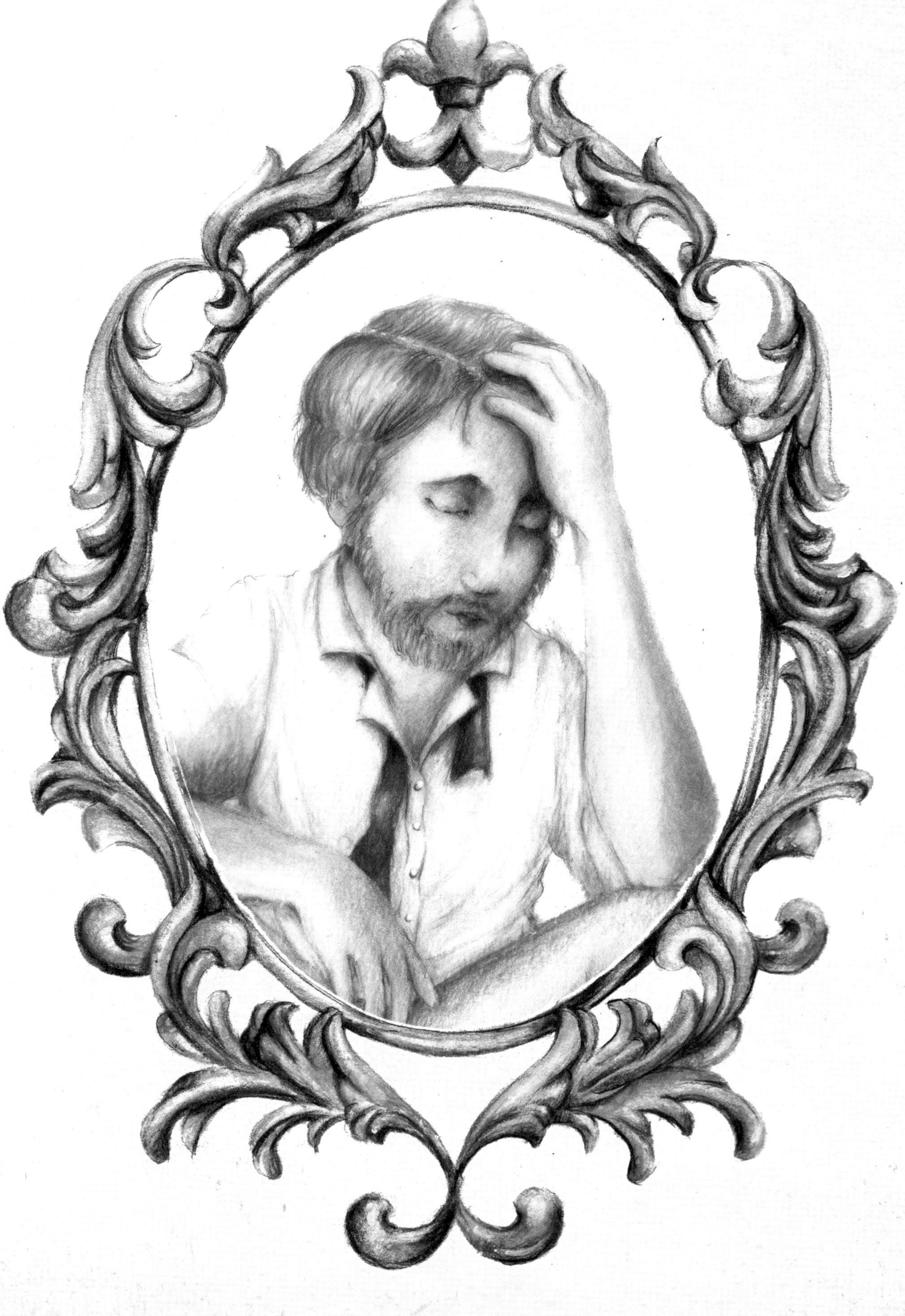

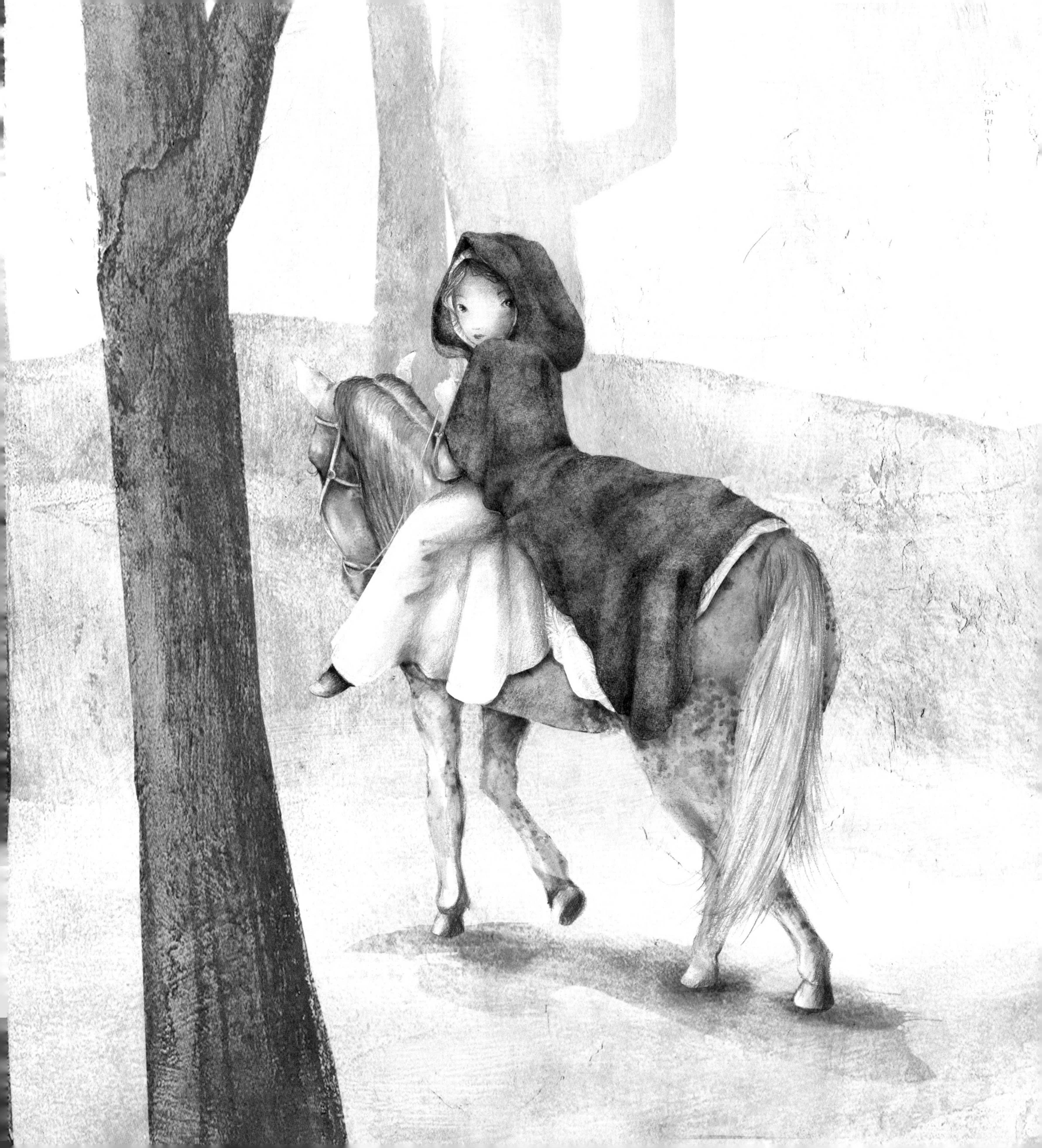

But the Beast couldn't stay mad at Belle for long, so after a while he agreed. "Very well, I'll let you go. But only if you promise to come back within a week. If you don't, I'll die from grief!"

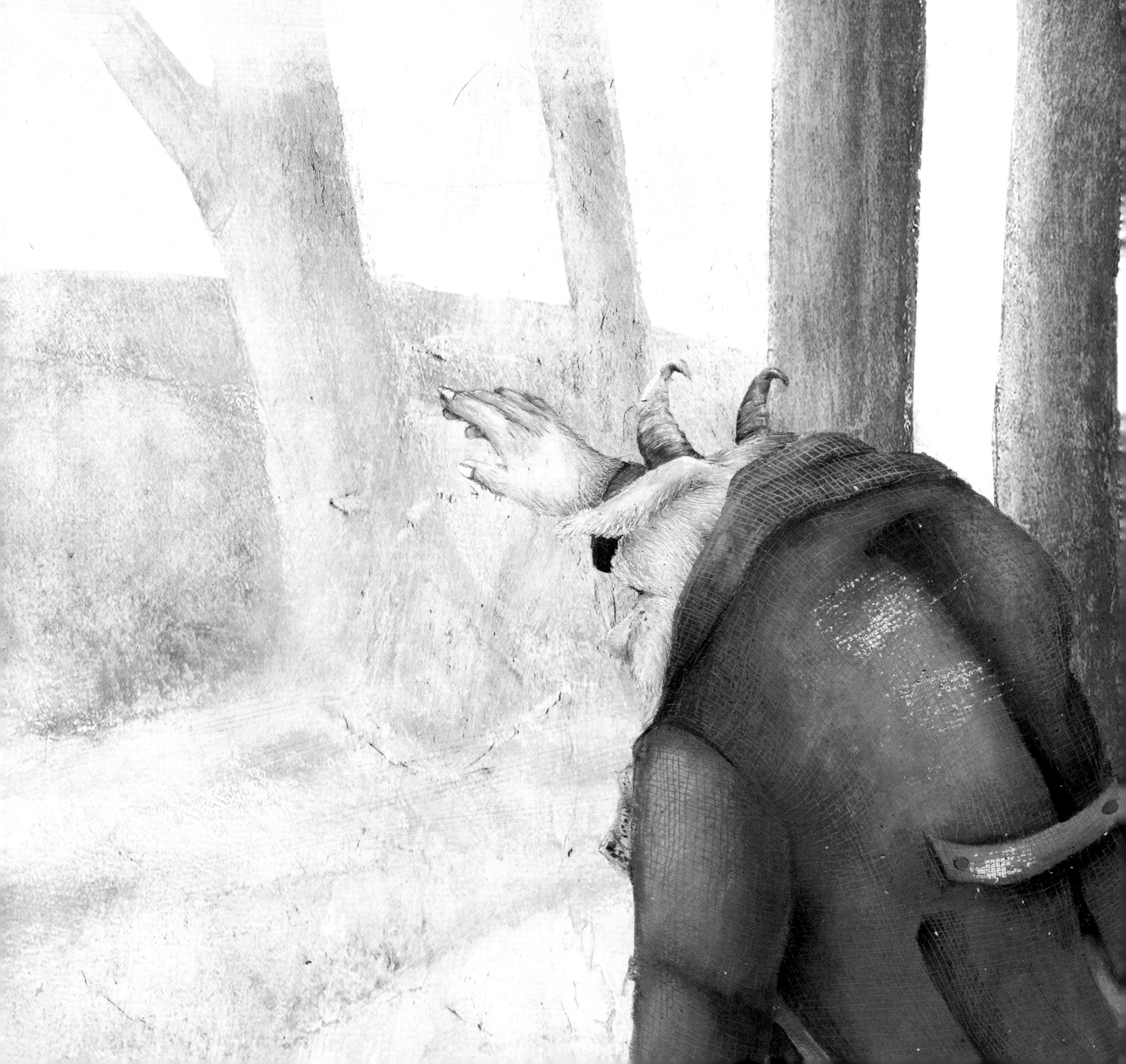

So Belle went home.

When her father saw her, he wrapped his arms around her and listened to her stories with a smile on his face. But her sister was green with envy. She couldn't bear the thought that Belle had such a nice life at the Beast's castle. "I'm the eldest and the prettiest," she grumbled to herself. "I should be living in a castle and wearing fancy dresses. Not Belle!" She came up with a cunning plan. *If I can't live in a beautiful castle, then Belle shouldn't either!* She thought. The night before Belle was to return to the castle, the conniving sister secretly put something in her drink that made Belle so sleepy that she slept all night and day.

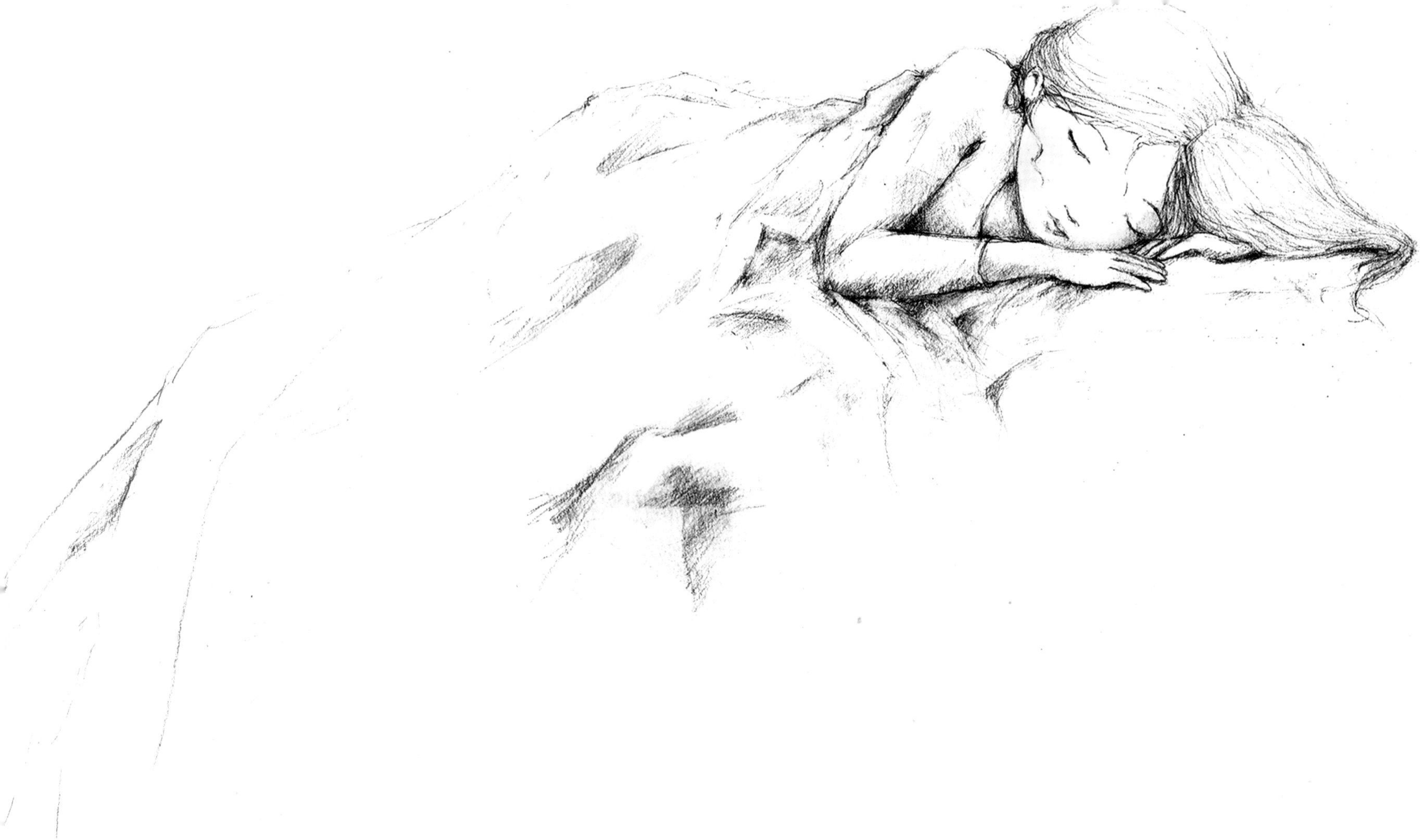

Belle dreamed the Beast was lying in his garden,
surrounded by his beloved roses. He wasn't moving…
She woke up bathed in sweat.

Her Beast!

She had to save him. Without saying goodbye
to her father and sister, she jumped on the horse
and rode like the wind to the castle.

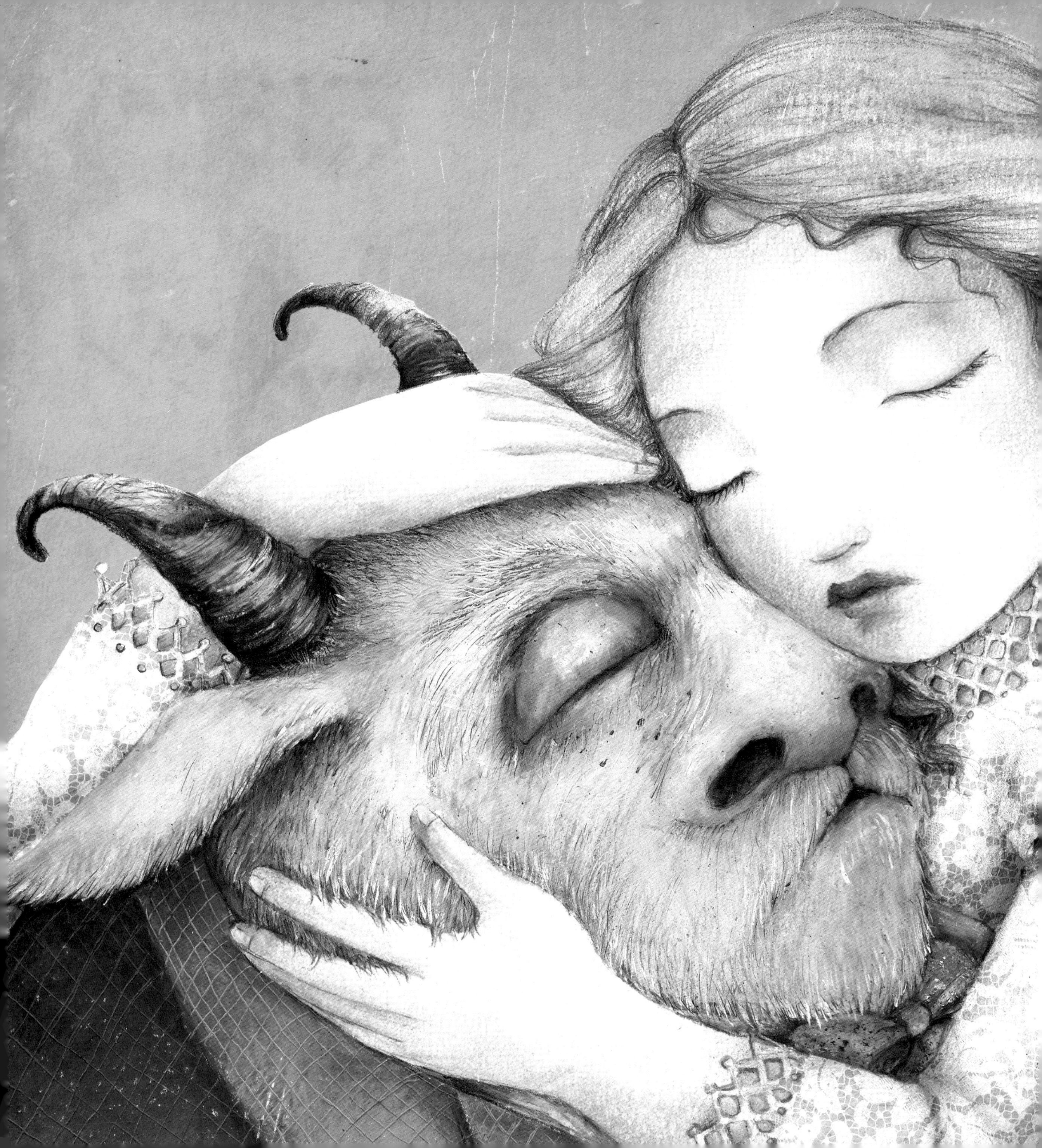

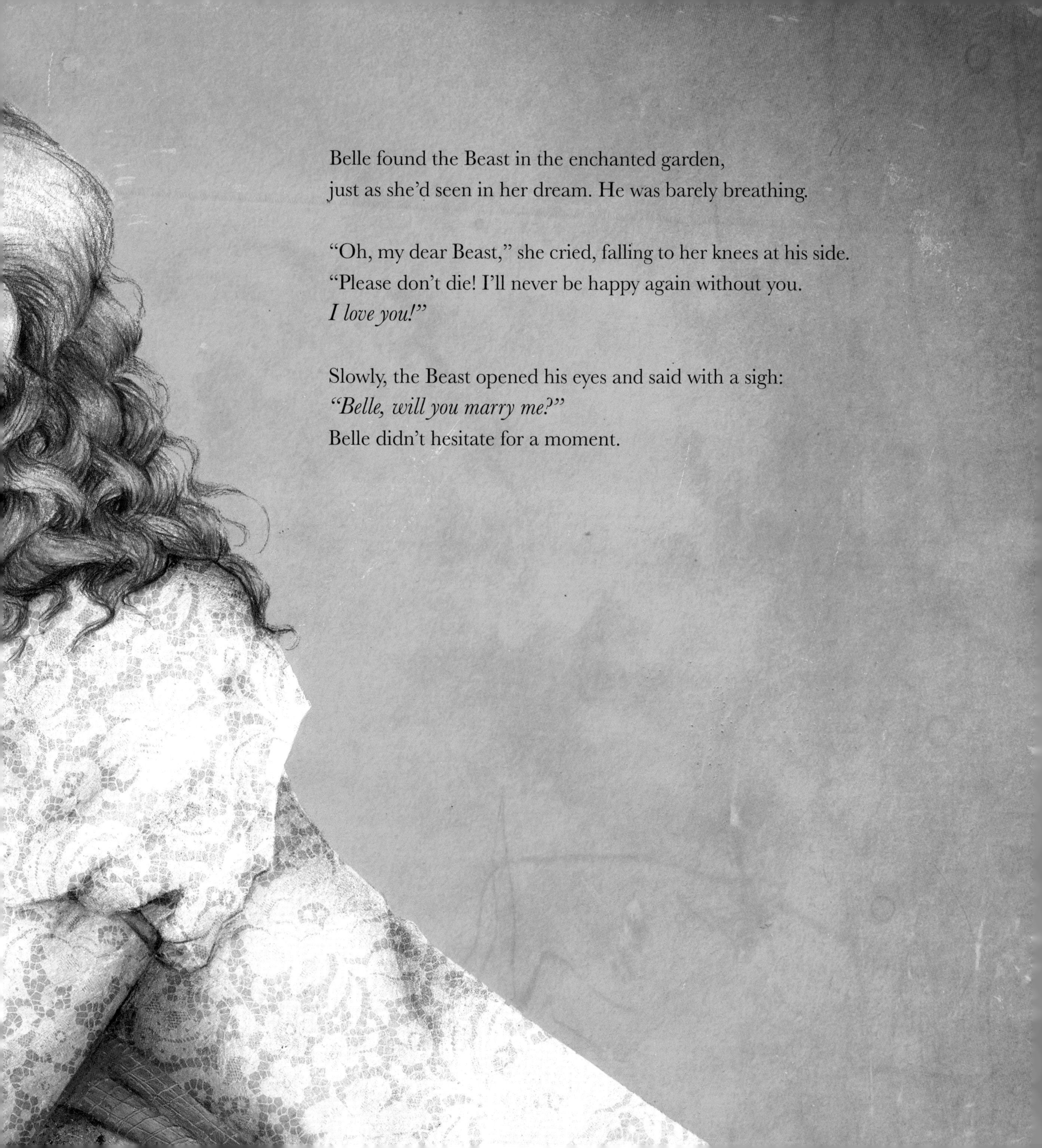

Belle found the Beast in the enchanted garden,
just as she'd seen in her dream. He was barely breathing.

"Oh, my dear Beast," she cried, falling to her knees at his side.
"Please don't die! I'll never be happy again without you.
I love you!"

Slowly, the Beast opened his eyes and said with a sigh:
"Belle, will you marry me?"
Belle didn't hesitate for a moment.

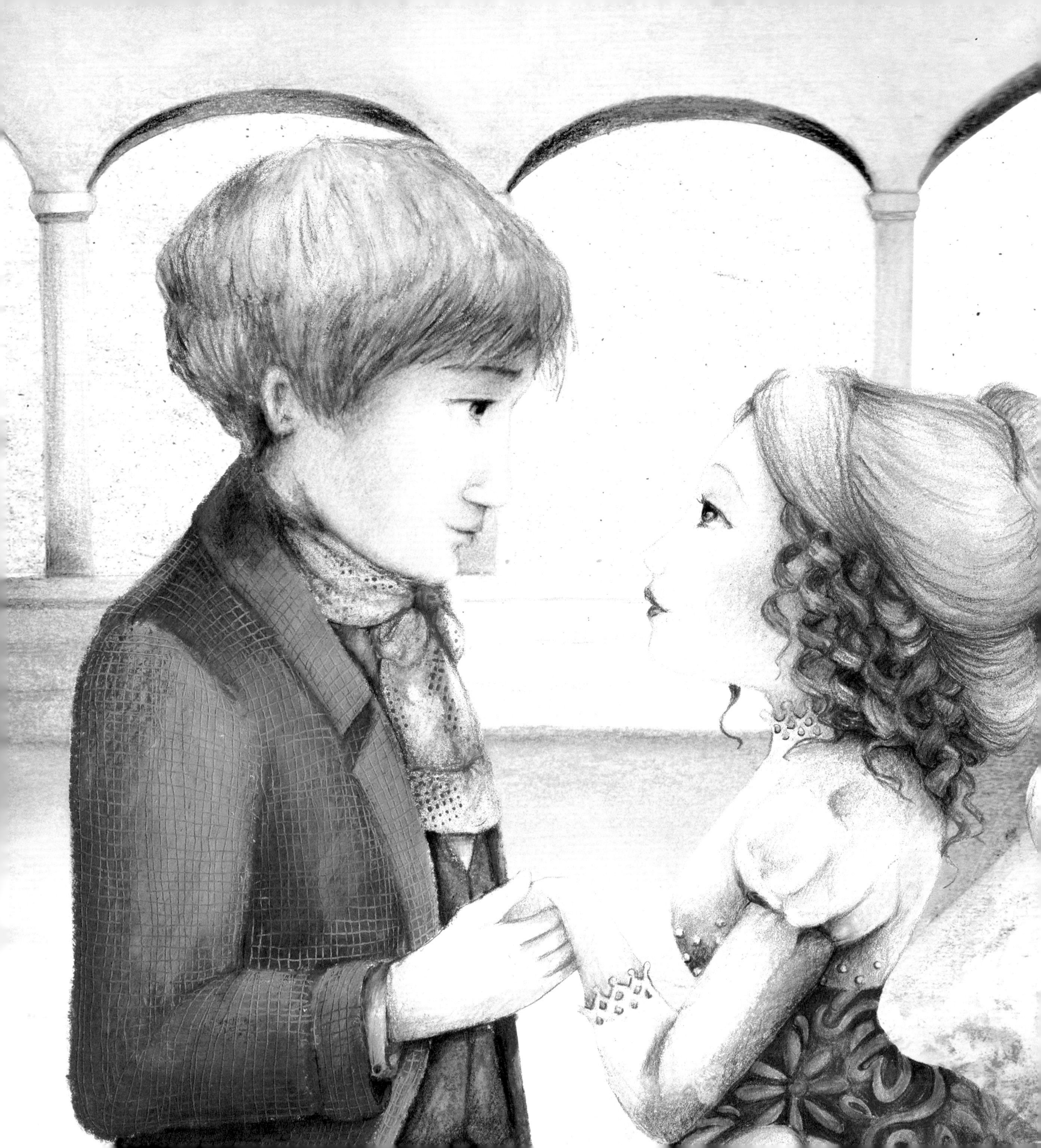

No sooner had Belle said "Yes!" than everything around them started to spin. Suddenly the garden was bathed in blinding light and when it disappeared, the Beast was gone too. A handsome prince was standing in front of Belle.

"My dear Belle, years ago an enchantress cast a spell on me and my castle to teach me a lesson. She changed me into a hideous Beast until I stopped thinking only of myself and someone would love me despite my looks."

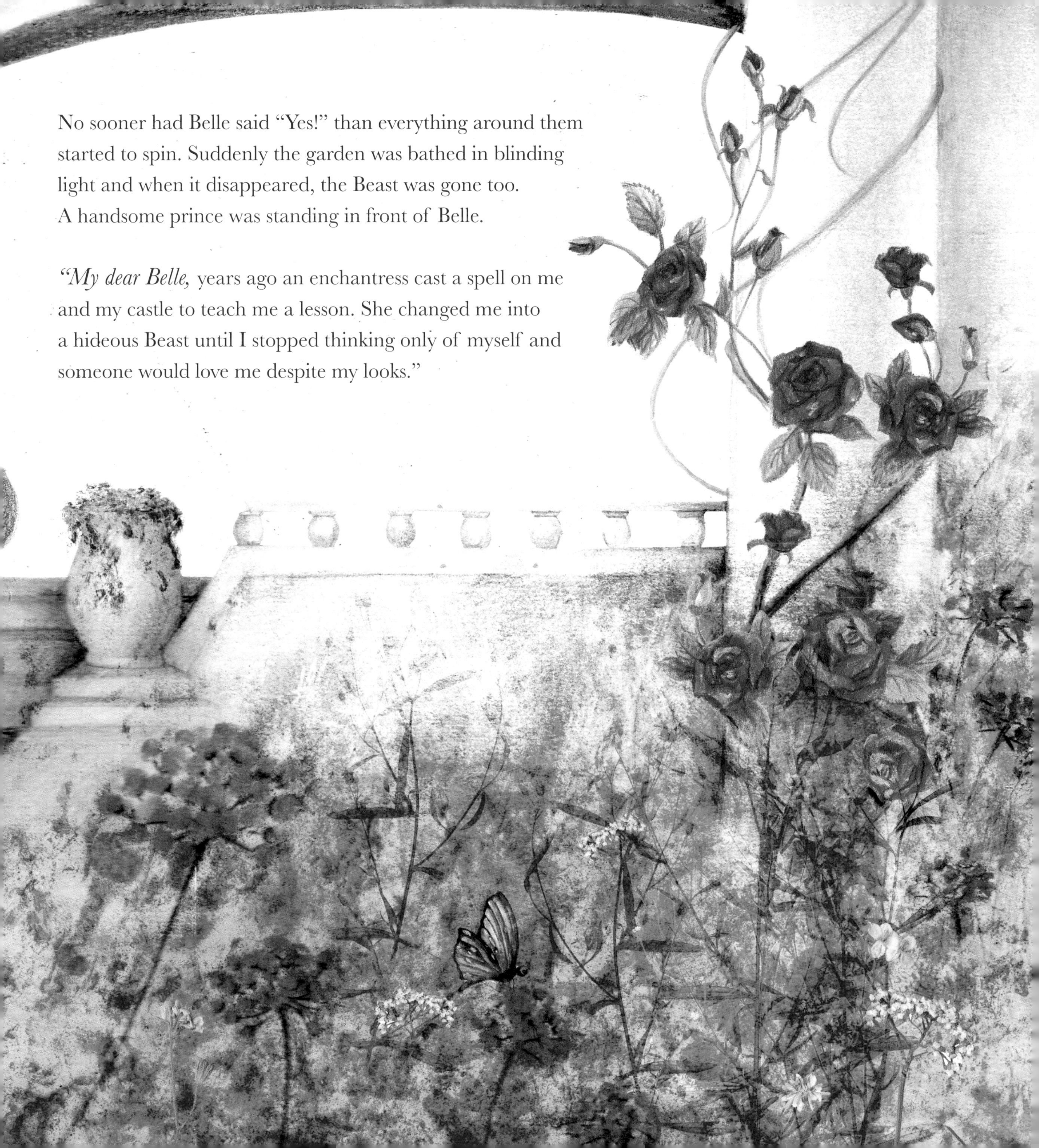

The next day, Belle married her prince.
The merchant and his eldest daughter came to the wedding. But when Belle's sister entered the castle and saw with her own eyes how dazzling it was, her jealous heart turned cold. She felt no joy for her sister.

The enchantress had witnessed everything, and she changed the elder sister into a statue as punishment. Belle's sister had to stand at the doors of the castle to witness Belle's happiness,

until one day a kind prince would come by to melt her heart…

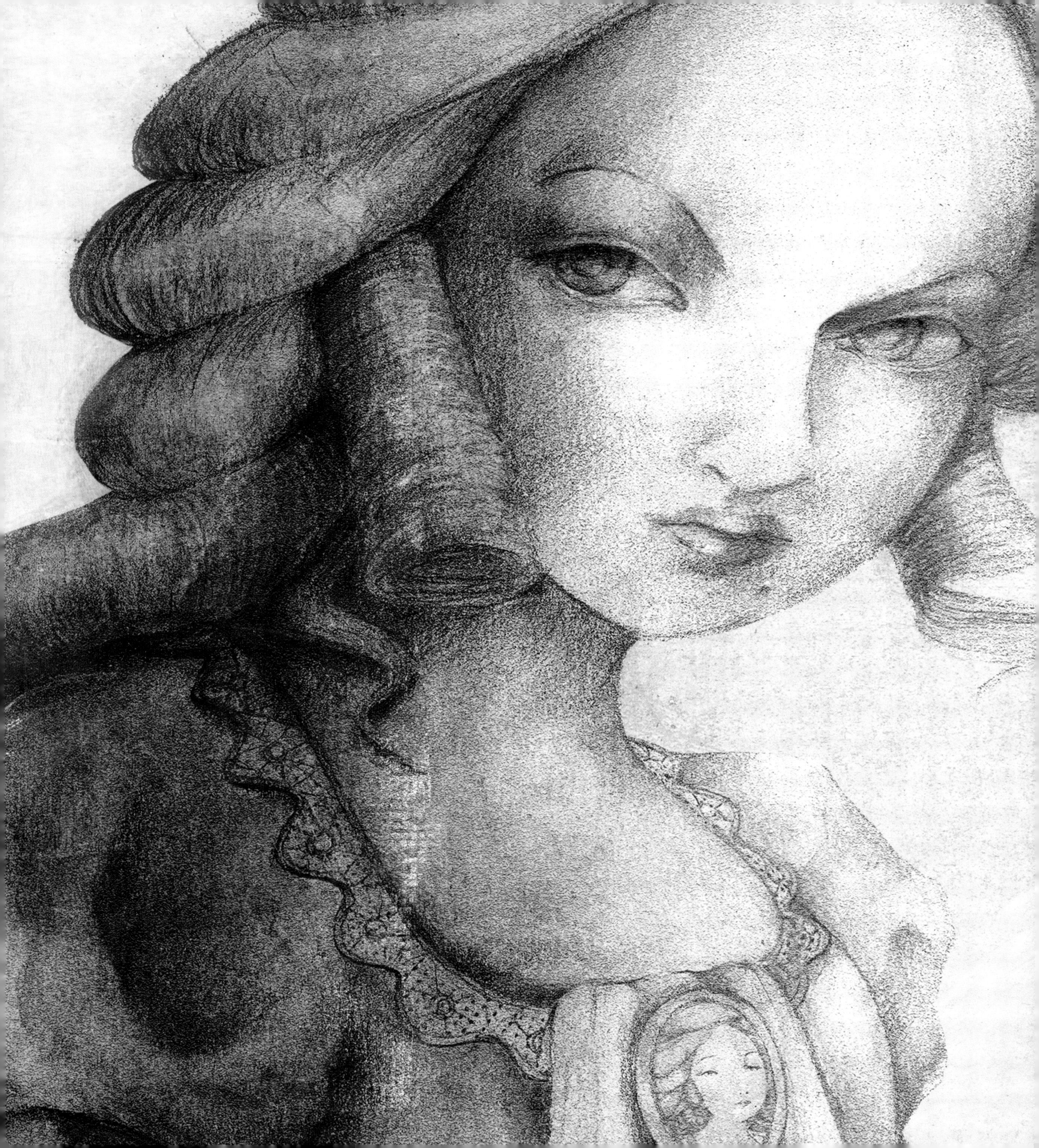

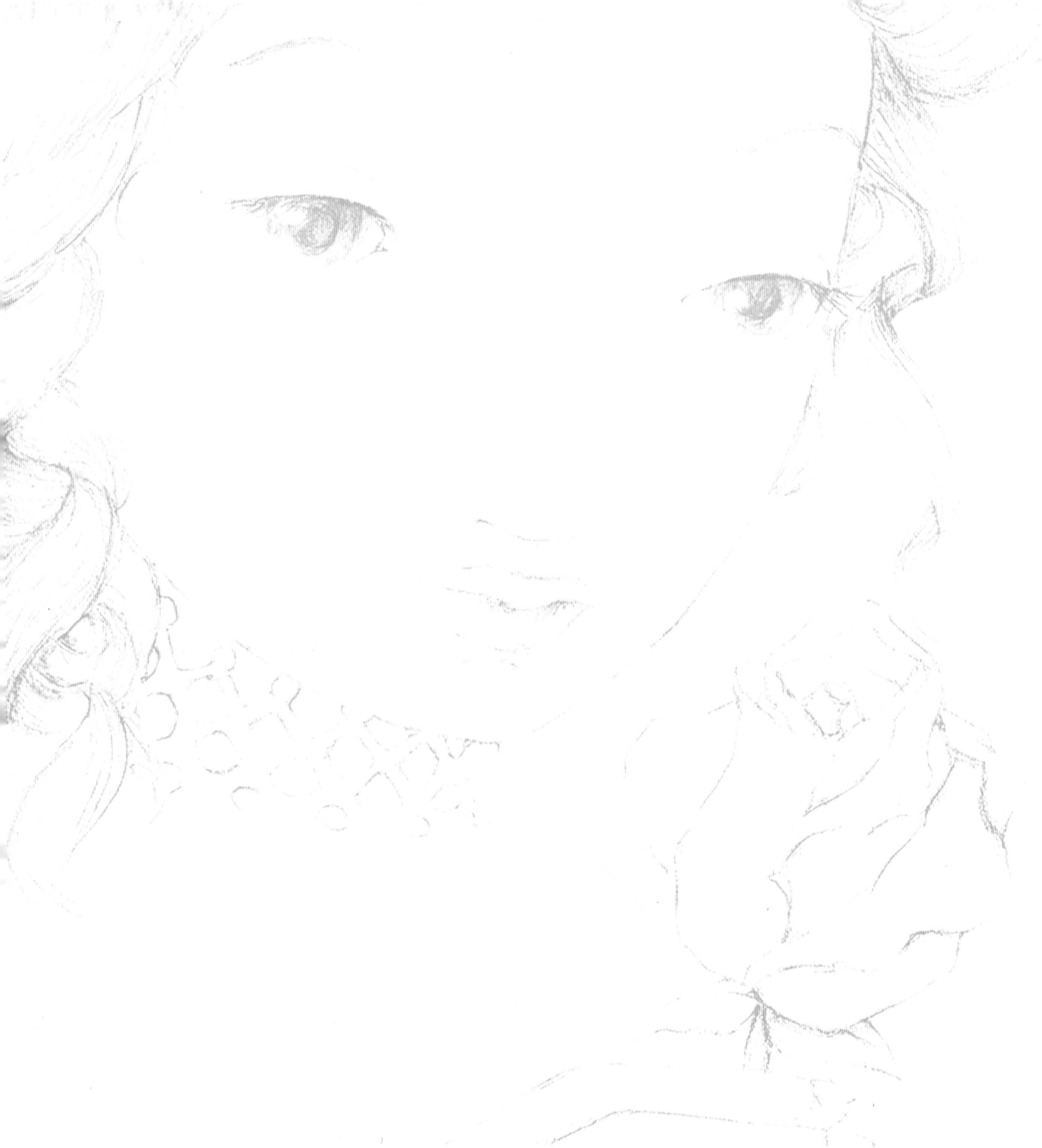